WHAT'S GOING ON
AT THE WHITLER?

WHAT'S GOING ON AT THE WHITLER?

ALISON MUKHERJEE

The Book Guild Ltd

First published in Great Britain in 2022 by
The Book Guild Ltd
Unit E2 Airfield Business Park,
Harrison Road, Market Harborough,
Leicestershire. LE16 7UL
Tel: 0116 2792299
www.bookguild.co.uk
Email: info@bookguild.co.uk
Twitter: @bookguild

Typeset in 11pt Minion Pro

Printed and bound in Great Britain by 4edge Limited

ISBN 978 1915122 742

British Library Cataloguing in Publication Data.
A catalogue record for this book is available from the British Library.

For David and Alison
who encouraged me
when I was ready to give up

CHAPTER ONE

Robert moves the salt and pepper onto the worktop and gives the table a good wipe. He doesn't give a toss about being tidy but he is most particular about keeping his flat clean. He washes and cleans everything he sets his eyes on. He's afraid that if he stops cleaning he'll end up like his mum who never cleaned anything if she could avoid it. Every surface in her kitchen was covered in grease, and globules of fat formed on the ceiling. The floor was slippery as an ice rink but instead of washing it, she covered the oily patches with sheets of newspaper. And no matter how filthy the dining table was, she simply spread a tablecloth over it to hide the dirt.

Robert's mum claimed she didn't have time to hoover and dust and clean like other women because she was too busy reading books from the library. She reckoned it took her on average two days to read a book, depending on the thickness, then a couple of hours to digest what she'd read before she started on the next one. She read biographies and travelogues and detective stories and thrillers and romances, she read anything that helped her forget the terrible mistake she made when she married Robert's dad.

One day stands out clearly in Robert's memory. He'd climbed onto the kitchen stool with the intention of raiding the biscuit tin when he noticed a line of tiny footprints etched into the layer of fat covering the base of the frying pan. He climbed down again and went off in search of his dad.

'Come and see what I've found.' He dragged his dad into the kitchen. 'A giant spider walked across our frying pan!'

His dad examined the evidence. 'Not a spider, son. Those prints were made by a mouse. Go and call your mum. Tell her there's something she's got to see.'

Robert had to repeat his message three times before his mum put down her book and followed him into the kitchen.

'What's all the fuss about?'

Robert's dad thrust the frying pan under his wife's nose. 'A bleeding mouse has walked across the bleeding frying pan and you ask what the fuss is about?'

Robert's mum's response was to put the frying pan on the hotplate so the fat melted and the tracks disappeared. Satisfied she'd removed all trace of mouse, she tossed in some sausages and rashers of bacon and fried them crisp and seemed genuinely surprised when Robert and his dad refused to eat them. That night Robert lay in bed wondering whether the scuffling, tapping noises that filled the darkness came from overflowing gutters or an infestation of vermin.

Robert grew up without friends. No one wanted to sit beside him in the classroom or kick a ball around the streets with him or go back to his place for tea. That's not surprising; his mother rarely put him in the bath or washed his clothes and rumour had it that if you stepped inside his house for more than five minutes the germs would kill you.

In any case Robert didn't have time for friends. With his dad in and out of prison like a yo-yo and his mum busy filling the house with germs and books, it was left to Robert to keep the show on the road.

He made sure there was food in the fridge and enough tokens to satisfy the electric meter; he kept a diary of when his dad was due in court and saw to it he was dressed for the part; he came home from school in lunch break to remind his mum to take her tablets. It wasn't till much later, when he moved into his own place, that Robert realised what he did wasn't normal, that being responsible for his parents meant he missed out on being a child.

Robert fills a jug and dribbles water over the collection of cactus plants on the windowsill, slowly so the parched compost has time to absorb the liquid. When he rescued them from his mum's bungalow last year, the plants were shrivelled up and stunted. He repotted them in cactus-friendly compost and fed them nutrients and minerals and now they've doubled in size. Some are in flower, brilliant red and gold blossoms bursting directly from the plant's bulbous, spikey limbs without bothering to wait for stems.

He read somewhere that cactus plants come into flower at significant points in their owner's life. Well, his dad died at the end of last year followed by his mum six months later, you can't get more significant than that! Now Robert owns the plants and he's planning to make significant changes to his life too, though not quite so drastic obviously. He hasn't decided exactly what he'll change, take a year out to travel abroad perhaps, move house or change jobs… yes, that would be a good place to start, a new job. Now that he's buried both his parents Robert's on the lookout

3

for something more exciting than the factory where he's worked for twenty years making plastic bottles from the by-products of refining oil. The job is boring, in fact it's so bloody boring Robert sometimes falls asleep while he's doing it. He would like a job which involves taking risks. A challenge, an adventure, a chance to prove he's got what it takes.

* * *

Tia is not easily fazed. She's the sort of person who can do five or six different things at the same time and do them well. Her chapatis are all exactly the same size, each one a perfect circle, and her fried rice is never stodgy. You could eat your dinner off her kitchen floor it's so clean. Her clothes are always a perfect fit, neither tight nor baggy, and there's something about her body chemistry which keeps her gold ornaments shining as brightly as they did when they were new. She raised two children virtually single-handed while holding down an admin job with the City Council. And yet when her son, Subir, asks her to look after her granddaughter Bindu during half-term, Tia is filled with dismay.

'We've left it a bit late this year and the childminder is fully booked. You're okay to help us out aren't you, Ma?' Subir prizes the top off the cake tin.

Tia reaches for her diary. 'I'm pretty busy that week. The usual three days at the Gallery, dentist on Wednesday and reading group Friday morning.'

'We need you the whole week. Monday through to Friday.' Subir puts his arm round Tia's shoulders and pulls her close. There's no other feeling quite like it, her son openly expressing his affection.

'Can't you take annual leave? After all, Bindu is your only granddaughter. You're always complaining you don't see enough of her.'

That may have been true in the past but not anymore. Although she would never say so to Subir, in Tia's opinion Bindu is a spineless whinging, whining child and the last thing Tia wants to do is spend a whole week in her company.

It hasn't always been like this. Tia was delighted when Bindu was born. The mass of dark hair, the bewildered eyes, the fragile fingers and pea pod toes. This tiny, brand-new human life which a few moments ago did not exist, now lay warm and snuffling in Tia's arms. She had seen the ultrasound scans, she had watched the foetus punch and kick the walls of Putul's bulging womb, but nothing could prepare her for this miracle. The baby came to them pure and untarnished, as if from outer space and as Tia held her for the first time, anything seemed possible. It didn't last, Bindu soon lost her innocence and became enmeshed in the web of cause and effect, action and reaction which binds each human being to countless others.

Putul was pretty much wiped out when she brought Bindu home and Subir had to return to work, so for the first few weeks Tia took full responsibility for Bindu's care; bathing, burping, bottle feeding and bundling her into the buggy for a spot of fresh air. While Bindu's father was busy seeing patients in his hospital clinic and her mother lay in bed recuperating or draping herself across the settee enjoying 'me time', granddaughter and grandmother were busy bonding. Bindu's eyes followed Tia round the room and she squirmed and fretted until she was in her grandmother's arms, which gave Tia enormous satisfaction.

Tia had always assumed that Subir would ask her to take care of Bindu when Putul returned to work. She even warned her line manager at the Whitler Gallery she would most likely be putting in for early retirement so she could look after the child – though she'd never quite convinced herself that was really what she wanted to do. Then one Saturday morning Subir announced they'd found an excellent (and very expensive) nursery with a vacancy and that Bindu would be starting there next month.

'Going to nursery will teach her to be strong and independent. She'll learn how to stand on her own feet,' Subir quoted the nursery's marketing material.

'*Hore Ram!* Dear God! The child's only six months old!'

'It's never too early,' Putul chipped in. 'We want our daughter to have the best possible start in life.'

Tia told them very firmly that in her opinion nothing could give a child a better foundation than being looked after by her own Thakuma. But they wouldn't change their minds no matter how much she tried to persuade them. That was seven years ago. Since then, Tia has had little say in the way her granddaughter is raised; well, she has plenty to say but no one listens.

And now here is Subir asking Tia to take time off work to look after Bindu, implying any reluctance on Tia's part proves that her first allegiance is to the Gallery with Bindu coming a poor second.

Tia hears herself say, 'I suppose I could have a word with Lucy. We don't have anything urgent on right now. And the dentist was only a check-up…'

Tia is not one to spend the week complaining. She'll approach half-term as an opportunity to develop a rapport with Bindu, perhaps even turn her into the kind of granddaughter she can be proud of.

* * *

The next time Robert has a day off, he drops into the jobcentre on the high street, behind the main post office. He studies the little cards pinned on the noticeboard, advertising vacancies. Cleaner, admin worker, HGV driver, care assistant, shelf stacker, bricklayer's assistant. None of them comes anywhere close to meeting his criteria. The young woman behind the desk asks Robert if he needs any help. Her fluffy blonde hair surrounds her face like a halo and her cheeks flush as she speaks. She doesn't look old enough to leave school, never mind offering help to a bloke his age. Of course looks can deceive. People often think Robert is much younger than he actually is. His arms and legs move with a clumsy eagerness which gives the impression of youth.

'Would you like to make an appointment to talk to one of our advisers?' She approaches him cautiously. 'If you're free right now, we've just had a cancellation.'

He says yes, he would like to speak to someone and yes, he is free right now. She shows him into an interview room no larger than a monk's cell and gives him a stack of leaflets to read while he's waiting. He leafs through them and discovers he's too old to join the fire service but could apply to the army or the police force. Both would meet his criteria in terms of excitement. On the other hand, both involve serious study, attending lectures and passing exams and he's no good at that stuff.

The adviser, when he comes, is not much older than the young woman on reception. He's wearing a jacket and tie but looks as if he would be more comfortable in tracksuit bottoms and trainers. He reeks of aftershave and he chews his nails.

'Hello there! My name is Craig. I look after our more mature customers so I'll be working with you this morning. Is it okay if I call you Robert?' He doesn't wait for a reply. 'So, you're looking for a job, Robert. Is that right?'

Obviously it's right; why else would he have come to the jobcentre?

'Let's start with your employment history.'

Robert looks blank.

'Can you tell me something about the different jobs you've done up till now?'

Robert tells Craig that he's worked in the same factory ever since he left school.

'Qualifications?'

Robert shakes his head. 'I didn't get round to handing in the course work and I'm no good at exams.'

'Transferable skills?'

Robert doesn't know what that means.

'On the job training?'

Robert has done bits and pieces of training over the years but can't remember the details.

'What kind of things do you like doing? What kind of things are you good at?'

Robert's palms begin to itch, which often happens when he's nervous. If he says 'cleaning' Craig will have him mopping floors and if he says 'looking after cactus plants' Craig will stick him in a garden centre.

Craig smiles patiently. 'Let's start again. I don't think you're known to us, are you? I thought not. I can't find you on the system. So we need to start by getting you registered.' Craig pops out of the interview room and makes a 'we've got a right one here' face for the benefit of the young woman who giggles into her laptop.

He sorts out the relevant forms and hands them to Robert. 'They shouldn't take too long to complete. Give me a shout when you finish. I'm just next door.'

This is not what Robert anticipated. He called in to speak to somebody, not to do a mound of paperwork. He's no good at paperwork. He perseveres for ten minutes then decides to quit. On his way out he asks the young woman to tell Craig he's changed his mind. She follows him to the door.

'Wait! Please! I need to know why you're leaving.' She looks as if she's about to burst into tears. 'Can you fill in this customer satisfaction survey? And this is the form if you want to make a complaint.' She thrusts a bundle of paper into his hand.

Robert waits till he's put a considerable distance between himself and the jobcentre before shouting, 'Stuff your frigging forms! If that's the best you can come up with, I'm better off on my own.'

He walks home to save the bus fare and on the way it strikes him – the obvious solution. He'll follow in his dad's footsteps and stick two fingers up at the law! Robert's dad dealt in wholesale counterfeit goods, fraudulent insurance claims, charity scams and any other trick that came his way.

He never said no to a deal of any kind so long as it didn't hurt the small guy. It's a world Robert knows well, a world where you are never more than one careless move away from being arrested, where you have to think quickly and keep an eye out for the enemy. Robert adopts a swagger, rolling his hips and swinging his arms. When he opens the door to his flat everything seems more cheerful than he remembers; the flowers on the curtains are a brighter pink and the walls a more brilliant white.

The euphoria lasts until it comes to making a decision about which particular line of criminal activity he'll get involved in. Robert draws up a list of possibilities and then considers them one by one. He can't see himself robbing a jeweller's shop or a post office or a bank; he'd never carry it off. He could sell substandard goods but then he'd have to cope with angry customers. He wouldn't touch drugs or people-trafficking with a barge pole, that would be taking advantage of the poor and helpless. The smart thing to do would be to hack into computers and steal personal data but he doesn't know how. There's no point in worrying. Something will turn up. It's a case of keeping his eyes and ears open.

* * *

Subir is supposed to be dropping Bindu off outside the leisure centre. He's already ten minutes late. Tia herself is never late and never misses an appointment. It's difficult to tolerate others' shortcomings when you have so few yourself. She takes a seat on the bench overlooking the slip road so she can watch the cars coming in. Everywhere mothers and fathers are securing babies in buggies and hauling sports bags out of car boots, while excited older children run on ahead. Tia can't imagine Bindu getting excited, she's more likely to refuse to get out of the car.

A car park attendant strolls over. 'Waiting for someone?'

'My son and granddaughter.' Tia consults her watch. 'They should have been here fifteen minutes ago.'

'Probably caught up in traffic. The motorway is very slow this morning.' The attendant shades his eyes and peers at the line of cars queueing up to enter the car park. 'What are we looking for?'

'Handsome, tall, slim. A good head of hair.'

'I meant the car!' They both laugh. 'You'll get cold sitting there. Best wait inside. If you tell me what make and model I'll keep an eye out and let them know where you are.'

'That's very kind of you but I'd rather stay here.'

By the time Bindu and Subir finally show up they are forty minutes late. In spite of her annoyance at being kept waiting, Tia feels the familiar surge of pride mixed with tenderness. A feeling which is quickly replaced by irritation and despair at the sight of Bindu dragging herself miserably in his wake.

'Sorry if we've kept you waiting.'

Tia wonders what he means by 'if'? There's no 'if' about it!

'Getting her ready took longer than I expected.' Subir tousles Bindu's hair indulgently. 'She couldn't make up her mind whether to wear her black jeans or the blue ones. Then it took Putul an age to get breakfast into her. You're not a morning person are you, *shona*?'

A morning person? For goodness sake. She's seven years old! She should fit in with the rest of the family, like it or not.

'Never mind. You're here now.' Tia touches her son's cheek. 'You're looking tired, Baba. Are you eating properly?' She knows better than to ask if Putul is feeding him well.

'I'm fine, don't fuss.' He hands Bindu's designer rucksack to Tia. 'What are your plans for today?'

Tia is ready for this. They're going swimming and that's final, but she won't tell Bindu until after Subir has left in case the child raises objections. From the start Subir and Putul have had this thing about allowing Bindu to choose. Just imagine, asking a little baby what flavour yoghurt she'd like for lunch or what colour Babygro she wants to wear that morning! Now she's older, Bindu's absolute right to choose affects the whole family. They'll be all ready to go on a trip to the seaside when Bindu changes her mind and wants to go up into the hills. Or they'll be settling down in an Italian restaurant when Bindu decides she prefers Chinese. Although, to be honest, Tia has noticed that nine times out of ten Bindu's parents persuade her to do what they wanted to do in the first place, which only confuses the child still further. Whenever Tia raises this with Subir, he tells her to butt out.

'We'll find something to do,' she looks at Bindu, 'won't we?'

Bindu stares at Tia but doesn't reply. They walk over to the leisure centre together, Bindu tucked into her father's side. Subir comes to a halt when they reach the entrance.

'I must get going. Look. I've put her inhaler here, in the outside pocket.' Subir taps the spot. 'She knows how to use it.' He stoops to give Bindu a quick hug. 'Bye then, see you tonight.'

'Don't leave me here,' Bindu screeches, clinging to her father's sleeve. 'Take me with you. Please.'

'Hey, what's this about? You'll be fine with Thakuma.'

'Of course she will. We're going to have fun!' Tia does a brilliant impression of enthusiasm.

Subir frees himself from his daughter's clutches. 'I'll keep my phone switched on. You can get in touch any time.' Bindu continues to wave until he's out of sight but he doesn't look back.

'*Chollo*. Come on! Let's go and get changed. We're going into the pool!' Tia reaches out to take Bindu's hand.

Bindu doesn't move. She forms her lips into a pout. 'I don't like the pool. It smells nasty.'

'That's chlorine. They have to put it in the water to stop infections spreading. It kills the germs.' Tia grabs Bindu's hand. '*Chollo*. Hurry up or we won't get a locker.'

'It makes my skin itchy.'

'Not if I rub you all over with barrier cream. Look! I've brought some with me.'

'It makes my hair smell.'

'You can keep your head out of the water.'

'I want to phone Mummy. She's doesn't make me do things if I don't want to.'

The lad on reception is watching with amusement, waiting to see what happens next. Taking their cue from him, the families at the front of the queue turn their heads. Tia announces that she's going inside. If Bindu doesn't want to come, that's fine, she can stay right where she is and Tia will collect her later. Tia begins to walk towards the changing rooms. Realising she is not going to get her own way, Bindu races to catch up.

Once they're in the changing cubicle Bindu continues to do whatever she can to sabotage Tia's plans, straining her grandmother's patience to the limit in the process.

'My costume is still wet from last time.'

'It feels wet because it's cold, in fact it's perfectly dry.'

'I've got a scratch. I can't go into the pool with a scratch.' She shows Tia a tiny graze on her forearm.

'I'll cover it with a plaster. I always carry one or two in my bag.'

Eventually grandmother and granddaughter emerge from their cubicle and paddle through the foot bath into the pool area. All around children are enjoying themselves, playing on floats, sliding down the chute and swimming through each other's underwater legs. Their screams of delight echo in the moist air. Bindu elects to go to the shallow end where mothers with young children congregate. She stands at the side of the pool, whimpering and refusing to let go of the handrail even though the water barely reaches her knees.

Tia tries to work out how Bindu contrives to look so pathetic. The proportions of her face are good, a broad forehead, big almond eyes and full lips. She's not ultra-skinny like some girls of her age, nor is she overweight. There's nothing wrong with her face or her figure, it's her scowl and the way she holds herself – shoulders hunched and knees bent – that are the problem. You might think she's trying not to be noticed and yet you sense she wants you to notice that she's trying not to be noticed.

'Come over here beside me.' Tia whisks a spray of droplets in Bindu's direction.

'I'm cold. I want to get out.'

'You're cold because you're not properly in the water. Let's go a little deeper, then you can show me how well you can swim.'

'I don't want to swim.'

Tia's friend Shompa waves at her from the other side of the pool. Her two grandsons are with her, splashing and play-fighting and having fun like normal children. Tia returns the wave.

'If you don't want to swim then come with me and you can play with Shompa granny's grandsons.'

'I'm cold. I don't want to play. I want to get out.'

It's only Monday and Tia's already very close to missing the first target she set herself – i.e. not to lose her temper however much she's provoked.

'Okay, you stay here. I'm going over to say hello. I won't be long.'

'No! Don't leave me. You mustn't leave me!'

Bindu lets go of the handrail and lunges towards Tia, misses her footing and lands with some force on her knees. Tia helps her to her feet and inspects the damage; mercifully there are no cuts or grazes, only a small sore patch on her right elbow which promises to turn into a bruise. A little huddle of bathers forms, brimming with sympathy for Bindu and hostility towards Tia.

'You're lucky she didn't crack her head on the edge as she went down.'

'She's been miserable from the start. Why did you bring her when she doesn't like being in the water?'

Too embarrassed to argue, Tia leads the way back to the cubicles.

* * *

A sudden loud knock on his front door jolts Robert out of his reverie. For a moment he's convinced – even though he knows it's not possible – that he's been thinking aloud and that whoever is at the door knows all about his plans to pursue a career in crime.

The flap of the letter box opens. 'Hello. Hello. Anyone there?'

'Be with you in a moment.'

Robert has a quick look at his reflection as he passes the hall mirror. His face is basically round. The bridge of his nose sits in a deep groove giving him a stoved in kind of look, he gets that from his dad. He has a few wrinkles on his forehead and there's the beginnings of a double chin. It's an average sort of face, neither so ugly nor so handsome as to stand out in a crowd. Robert finger-combs his hair into some kind of order and opens the door.

It's Jamie, the student from four doors down. Dickhead! Giving Robert a fright like that.

'Sorry to disturb you, mate. Did the postman leave a parcel here yesterday?' Jamie waves a delivery slip in Robert's face.

Of course! Robert remembers now. Leaving Jamie standing in the doorway, he fetches the parcel. 'More books?'

'Yep! Borrowing from the library doesn't work for me. I need my own copies. Second hand where possible.' Jamie peers over Robert's shoulder into the flat. 'What about you?'

Robert, defensively, 'What about me?'

'Do you buy books or borrow them?'

'Both.'

It's a lie. Robert never borrows anything from the library. But he does occasionally have a look round his local bookshop. Only the other day he bought a couple of books offering advice and guidance to men who are seeking to make changes in their lives, but that's his business not Jamie's.

It's obvious Jamie wants to prolong their chat and Robert humours him. Normally he wouldn't care but things have changed now that he's about to launch himself into the criminal world. While it's true he shouldn't be too pally with his neighbours, neither can he afford to get on the wrong side of them. One day they might be summoned to testify against him.

After a comprehensive but one-sided discussion of the weekend fixtures and the state of the transfer market – Jamie does all the talking – Robert looks at his watch and pretends to panic. 'Is that the time? Sorry, mate, have to make a phone call.'

'Thanks for looking after the parcel.' Jamie slouches off down the landing.

That evening Robert turns on the telly in the middle of a program about stolen works of art and is immediately hooked. Art was his favourite subject at school. He remembers with pride the project he did for Mr Marsh, the art teacher, in year twelve. They had to choose two artists, one modern and one from the Renaissance period, and compare them. Robert chose Leonardo da Vinci and Damien Hirst and compared the way they cut up bodies and that type of thing. The teacher gave him grade C, the highest mark he ever had in all his years at school. His mum was so proud of what he'd done she kept his project in a folder in the front porch and showed it several times over to the postman, the newspaper boy and the binmen.

According to the presenter, approximately 50,000 pieces of artwork are stolen every year, mostly on the spur of the moment, and only a small proportion are ever seen again. The thieves don't make money by selling their loot on the open market, the Art Loss Register has helped put an end to that; the value of the stolen masterpieces lies in their use as collateral to secure a loan or pay off a debt, in other words they are the currency of the criminal underworld.

The program goes on to discuss some high-profile cases in detail. The theft of Leonardo da Vinci's *Mona Lisa* from the Louvre in 1911 and the 1990 theft of thirteen pictures from the Isabella Stewart Gardner Museum, valued collectively at five hundred million dollars, the most famous heist of all.

The message of the documentary is that art theft is not a glamorous profession as many people mistakenly think; it's not a case of cultured individuals hiring someone to bring them a van Gogh so they can contemplate the masterpiece in their leisure time. It's actually all about greed and money. But this is not the message Robert hears. For him the programme reinforces his conviction that there is something cool and sexy about stealing a beautiful painting; being an art thief would earn him respect, show he has class. And just supposing he was sent down, he'd get preferential treatment from the screws because he was an art thief and not a common burglar.

So there you have it. Problem solved. Midlife change of career from factory worker to art thief! With the help of a dictionary Robert scribbles a one-line letter to his boss to say he's quitting his job at the factory.

One question still bothers Robert. He can't stand violence of any kind. He can't watch boxing on the telly and if he goes to the cinema he spends half the time with his eyes shut. Even watching the news can be a struggle. His mum occasionally clipped him round the back of the head but his dad never touched him in anger so it isn't a case of having bad memories. Why is he worrying? There's no reason to think dealing in stolen works of art should lead to anyone getting beaten up.

* * *

Back in the safety of the changing cubicles, Tia peels off Bindu's costume and wraps a towel around her shoulders. Bindu stands inert, her body stiff and unyielding through the cloth. Tia feels suddenly protective and gives her a quick hug.

'*Lokkhi meye*. Be a good girl and get yourself dressed.'

'You have to dry me. Mummy says I don't do it properly.'

'Then we'll show Mummy she's wrong.'

'I don't know how.'

Determined not to be riled, Tia concentrates on getting herself dressed. When she's finished, Bindu still hasn't moved. Tia retrieves the towel from the floor and without comment and perhaps a little roughly dries the bits of Bindu that haven't already dried out by themselves. She turns her attention to Bindu's hair, dragging the comb through the tangles. Despite early promise Bindu's hair is fine and lifeless and not even truly black. Her mother's genes, unquestionably.

'You're hurting me!' Bindu bats the comb away and claps her hands over her head.

Tia feels ashamed. It's not Bindu's fault her hair tangles easily. Tia has told Putul a hundred times that a scalp massage with coconut oil would do the trick but no one takes any notice.

'Mummy puts conditioner.'

'I'll remember next time.'

'I don't want a next time. I hate it here and I'm never coming again,' Bindu's eyes fill with tears.

On the way out they bump into Shompa. She suggests coffee while her grandsons mess about in the soft play area. Tia and Bindu follow her to a colourful plastic and vinyl space, full of screaming children, not the venue Tia would have chosen for a coffee but worth it if Bindu can make friends. They watch the boys scramble to the top of teetering towers and throw themselves down into ball pools. In spite of Tia's best efforts, Bindu refuses to follow their example.

'What is it with you and Bindu?' Shompa speaks quietly so that the children won't hear. 'Why don't you two get along?'

'You've seen for yourself. She's hard work.'

'I wonder if you're punishing her for being a girl.' Shompa, who has a reputation for frank speaking and homespun psychoanalysis, puts her head on one side and regards Tia through screwed-up eyes.

'*Jah*! What nonsense! I don't have a problem with Bindu being a girl. If a grandson behaved like she does I'd feel just the same.'

The thing is, Tia can't imagine a boy behaving like Bindu; boys are more likely to get up to mischief than to sulk (not a thought she's inclined to share with Shompa who would certainly accuse her of bias). Tia can cope with mischief but sulking infuriates her.

The boys complain they are hungry. Tia suggests they all go down to the Whitler Gallery Café for lunch. 'I'll take you down to the basement and show you my office if you like.'

Tia works in the archives section of the gallery, cataloguing the various documents handed in by members of the public, usually on the death of a relative, or by businesses when they refurbish or close down. She's pretty much her own boss, which is just as she likes it. Much more satisfying than trying to fit into a team of incompetents.

'Sorry, have to get back for the carpet man.' Shompa makes a sympathetic face. She knows Tia would prefer not to be left alone with Bindu. 'We're having the whole house done if we can afford it. Now boys, say goodbye to Tia auntie and Bindu didi. Lovely seeing you both.' She walks away, a grandson hanging on at either side.

Tia is suddenly overwhelmed with loneliness. Shompa is the perfect grandmother, unfailingly kind and loving, utterly devoted and yet full of fun. Tia was not like that even with her own children. Being at home never fully satisfied her. Perhaps if Tia had been more like Shompa, Subir wouldn't have chosen to attend a medical school at the other end of the country instead of living at home while he studied; and perhaps his sister wouldn't be living thousands of miles away in the United States. But Tia isn't like Shompa; Tia loves her children fiercely but not all-consumingly. She needs time and space for herself. You can't have it both ways.

* * *

Robert fetches a can from the fridge and tears back the ring. The Whitler Gallery is the obvious place to start looking. He's passed it many times. He's never actually been inside but his mum sometimes met her friends in the Whitler cafe. He knows the layout of the streets and how to get away quickly if he needs to. The Whitler is unlikely to have a complicated alarm system, the council doesn't have the money, another point in its favour.

So far as Robert knows, the Whitler doesn't have many really well-known paintings but that's not what he's looking for anyway. You can't sell a Rembrandt or a Turner direct to a collector, you have to go through a fence, who pays far less than the picture is worth. Robert needs to make a decent profit. Now that he has given up his job he'll have to live on his savings and they won't last long.

Robert scrolls down the online catalogue and quickly decides he wants something that looks like what it's supposed to be. In other words not a big orange splodge with the title 'summer holidays' or a black background with a few red dots called 'catching fish' or anything stupid like that. Portraits are good but nothing too modern. He eventually finds one that looks hopeful, an oil painting of Samuel Baker, a seventeenth-century businessman who grew up in the local area.

The picture shows a plump and kindly looking gentleman dressed in a velvet coat, with gold stitching on the cuffs and a long line of pearl buttons. Samuel holds a carved wooden stick in one hand and there's a coat of arms in the top right-hand corner of the picture to show his family is respectable. Apparently Samuel made his fortune in London and donated a generous sum of money to the city where he was born, for the purposes of founding a school. With any luck the school, which is now a top-notch private school, will join the gallery in paying a ransom in exchange for the return of the portrait of its founder.

As the plan begins to take shape, Robert can feel the adrenaline pumping. It's given him an appetite. He shoves his feet into trainers, grabs a jacket and picks up his house keys. He'll have lunch in the Whitler Gallery Café and have a good look round the building and find a way to get in and out without being seen. And check out the portrait of Samuel Baker – how big is it and how heavy, and how is it fixed to the wall? No good having everything in place and then finding at the last moment he can't get the bugger off the wall!

Robert has a spring in his step as he locks his front door and sets off down the landing towards the lift. The air is stale and there is no natural light. The lift when it arrives smells of dirty socks and rotten vegetables, but today Robert barely notices because this is the first day of his new career. He wishes he could tell someone, drop it casually into a conversation. What do I do for a living? Well, as a matter of fact, I steal works of art.

He shares the lift with Mr Stokes who lives at the other end of the landing and is permanently miserable. Mr Stokes stays inside when the sun shines in case he gets skin cancer, and when it rains he peers out of his window looking for signs of flooding. This morning he's convinced they're due for an exceptionally severe winter and that supplies of gas and electricity will run out. Robert looks at Mr Stokes and at the people he passes in the street and sees fear, boredom, weariness, resignation, lack of vision. Unlike them, Robert is going places. He plans to cut his teeth on the Whitler then move on to something more ambitious. Birmingham, Edinburgh, London, maybe even Paris and New York. For now though he must focus, attend to each detail, make sure everything goes smoothly on the day – or night – he hasn't yet decided which it's to be. He has to do his research first.

* * *

Tia decides it's not worth collecting her car from the multi-storey, so she and Bindu head off along crowded pavements to the Whitler Café for lunch. Bindu has an annoying habit of walking directly behind the person she's with and turning when they turn, so that she's permanently out of reach and out of sight. It's impossible to carry on a conversation like this, which is perhaps why she does it. Every so often Tia has to slow down or stop to let someone pass and Bindu crashes into her. Consequently she arrives at the Whitler exhausted and frazzled.

They stop briefly in the foyer to introduce Bindu to Evie who is managing the information desk. She makes a valiant effort but despite her extensive experience of working with the public, she can't coax even a shadow of a smile out of Bindu.

'If you're planning to eat in the cafe you'd better hurry. Look at the length of the queue! Oh, before you go, would you like to buy a raffle ticket? For the Children's Hospice.'

No, as it happens, Tia would not like to buy a raffle ticket. She's doesn't like donating to any cause until she's checked precisely what the money will be used for. But sometimes it's best to go with the flow. 'How much?'

'£1.00 each or £5.00 for a strip of six.'

Tia pays her dues then leads the way to the crowded café. As usual the hot meals smell appetising, hopefully there will be something Bindu likes. When they reach the front of the queue, they're directed to a corner table.

'What do you fancy – pasta, pizza, chips, chicken?'

Bindu mumbles something.

'What's that? Did you say curry?'

'I said I'm not hungry.'

Funny how the right to choose is always exercised by saying no rather than yes. 'Okay. Let's go for sandwiches. Egg or cheese or ham?'

'Not hungry.' Bindu puts her chin in her hands and gazes out of the window.

Tia buys two rounds of sandwiches, a coffee and a fruit juice. She tears open one of the boxes and begins to chew. The other box she slides towards Bindu who pushes it back again. If Putul was here she would beg and coax and cajole until Bindu eventually gave in and ate a few mouthfuls but Tia is not going to play that game. She drops the second box into her bag.

'We'll take yours with us, you can eat it later, but you must drink your juice.' It won't hurt Bindu to go hungry but Tia won't allow her to dehydrate.

While she eats, Tia observes other families. All the children are engaged in some kind of activity, eating or laughing or playing or squabbling. She can't see anyone withdrawn and silent like Bindu.

'How's school?'

'Okay.'

'Which subject do you like best?'

'None.'

'You mean you don't like any subjects?'

'I mean I don't have a favourite.'

'Which one do you get the best marks for then?'

'We don't get marks.'

Where does the child get it from, this infuriating refusal to co-operate, this constant need to go against the grain? Tia simply has to escape or she'll explode. She goes over to the counter to fetch a couple of paper napkins and strikes up a conversation with one of the waitresses while she's there. From across the room, Bindu's resentful gaze drills into Tia's skull.

The sky darkens. Drops of rain splash onto the pavement. Patrons seated in the garden hurry inside clutching the remains of their meal in one hand, their jackets and bags in the other. A young woman moves from table to table distributing leaflets containing details of the child-friendly activities currently on offer.

'Look! Making masks from papier mâché.' Tia gives Bindu an encouraging smile. 'That sounds fun. Or would you like to try origami?' Pause. 'Do you know what origami is?'

'Of course I know.' Bindu looks at Tia scornfully. 'It's folding paper into shapes. But I don't want to do it. I want to go home.'

'We're not going anywhere until the rain stops. If you don't want to go to the workshops then we'll have a look round the gallery.' Tia puts her hands firmly on Bindu's shoulders and steers her into the foyer. For once Bindu doesn't resist.

* * *

The Whitler Café is already crowded when Robert reaches it, and everyone except him has at least one child attached to them. He likes children and as a rule children tend to like him but he prefers them individually and certainly not in such large numbers. He doesn't want to waste time standing in the queue so he buys a bag of crisps to tide him over, then goes outside to study the exterior.

The first thing Robert notices is that there are no windows in the main building. The brickwork shows where the original windows were, but almost all of them have been blocked up. He supposes that's because they need all the wall space they can get for hanging the paintings. He had wondered about lowering the picture down from a window at the back but he may have to rethink that. There's only one entrance from this side. Surely there must be at least one more, most likely at the back, to comply with fire regulations. Robert wanders over towards the staff car park but discovers he can't get past the barrier without a code. He squints up at the surrounding buildings, searching for somewhere with a good view of the rear of the gallery. The multi-storey car park is worth a try; it's in the right position and it's open to the public. An elderly lady sidles up to him. She looks up, following the trajectory of his gaze and wonders what has attracted his attention.

'Rain on its way,' he says by way of explanation. 'Gardens could do with a good soaking.'

The woman gives him a strange look. It's November and they've had more than the average rainfall. He must be more careful!

Cutting across the shopping precinct and down the alley to the covered market brings Robert to the car park entrance. He feels like an imposter; he can drive but he's never owned a car. Taking the lift to the second floor, and pretending he's forgotten where he's parked, he moves to the outer edge and looks down. Yes, there it is. That's the Whitler Gallery. From above, the L-shaped outline is very clear. A van has driven right up close to the back of the café and someone is unloading boxes and trays – grocery supplies for the cafe no doubt. The entrance seems to be in constant use so is no help to him, at least not during the day.

Two women appear from nowhere and walk along the back of the building towards the staff car park. It's difficult to be sure from this distance, but it looks like there's a door at the far corner of the back wall. Intended for use by staff but also a good route out for Robert and the picture, assuming he can work out how to get to the door from inside.

A sudden gust catches Robert off guard prompting him to grab the grille with both hands. He's beginning to attract attention. There's no rational explanation for him being where he is unless he's planning to end his own life or damage one of the cars. It's started to rain so he pulls his jacket up over his head and sprints back to the Whitler to investigate.

* * *

Tia occasionally drops into the temporary exhibitions on the ground floor in her lunch break but, as is so often the case with things on her own doorstep, she's never made the effort to view the permanent collections on levels one and two. Her plan is to start at the top and work their way down.

The hustle and bustle of the cafe recedes as they follow the upwards curve of the marble staircase bordered by pure white walls and lit by art deco crystal chandeliers. There is no one else in the long, narrow Landscape Room but it doesn't feel empty. The collection of landscapes, water colours and oils, dating from the 19th century fills the space with windswept hills, dense forests and stormy skies. Tia and Bindu move round the room looking at each painting in turn. Landscapes without people or animals don't appeal to Tia. She prefers the flock of sheep on a mountainside surrounded by glistening snow, the herd of cattle drinking from a refreshing mill pool, or the maiden hand-on-hip in front of a picturesque thatched cottage.

'Which one do you like best?' Tia asks.

Bindu points to a picture of peasants driving their livestock along a country lane while a woman in a wagon nurses her child; an urban skyline traverses the far-off horizon.

'Why do you like it?'

'Dunno.'

Why did she waste her breath asking?

They proceed through the archway to the next room and come to an abrupt halt in front of a painting so large it covers one complete wall. Bindu covers her eyes with her palms.

'I don't want to look! It's scary. And it's rude.'

Tia concedes Bindu has a point. The mural shows a chaotic procession of nearly naked and almost certainly intoxicated figures, led by a well-built woman with legs like tree trunks. Mr Muscle is wrestling a snake and everywhere boobs pop out of bodices. One chubby cherub with pointed ears rides a leopard. Another is about to have his balls chewed off by a not so friendly goat! According to the label the picture is a 17th-century mural of Bacchus and Ariadne taken from on an original by Titian.

'It says here the picture is based on a Greek myth. Shall I read you the story?'

'No! Don't! I'll have bad dreams.'

Tia stands a while studying the mural. The colourful exuberance reminds her of the escapades of the Hindu gods and goddesses as told in the Puranas. The pot-bellied cherubs are not unlike Ganesh and the general party atmosphere is reminiscent of Lord Krishna dancing with the Gopis. There's even a chariot very similar to Arjun's.

Bindu tugs at the sleeve of Tia's jacket. 'I told you I don't like it.'

Tia insists on having a quick look at all the displays even though Bindu's restlessness makes it a constant battle. That's precisely how it feels, as if they're at war and fighting on opposite sides. If only they could agree on a truce or at least a temporary ceasefire. They are on the point of descending to level one when Tia notices a side room they've somehow missed.

Bindu groans. 'You promised! You said we could go home.'

'I said we could go when we've seen everything and we haven't seen this room. Look! It's called the Portrait Room. I think you'll find it interesting, but you can wait here while I pop in if you'd rather.'

Not wanting to be abandoned, Bindu grabs hold of Tia's arm and together they step inside the small, dimly lit space.

* * *

When Robert returns from the car park the Whitler Café is half empty. Pleased by his first attempt at surveillance, he orders an all-day breakfast with double sausage. He's developed quite an appetite so it doesn't take him long to finish his meal. Leaving a generous tip, he goes back into the foyer and joins the queue for the information desk. A waste of time as it happens because when his turn comes, the woman behind the desk directs him to the stack of leaflets displayed on a nearby stand.

'The gallery is running a raffle to raise money for the Children's Hospice, can I interest you in a ticket?' She catches Robert's eye. '£1.00 each or £5.00 for a strip of six – that's one for free.'

Does he look as if he can't work that out for himself?

Robert pays for the raffle tickets and stuffs them into his pocket along with a selection of leaflets from the stand, one of which contains a floor plan of the gallery which should be useful.

The Wildlife Photographer of the Year exhibition is worth seeing. Spectacular shots of giant spiders swallowing whole frogs, a baby deer so well camouflaged it takes five minutes to spot, a polar bear stranded on an island of melting ice. While parents exclaim over the photographers' skill their children roll round on the floor play-fighting, in imitation of the photographs of lion and tiger cubs which hang above them.

Robert wants to check the position of the CCTV cameras so he can steer clear of them but isn't sure how to do so surreptitiously, without attracting attention. He can't just stare up at the ceiling like he'd done outside a little earlier, so he snatches a series of fleeting glances but it's no good, he can't make sense of what he sees. A bit of ingenuity is called for; he pretends there's something in his eye and makes a big fuss of rolling his eyeball up and down a few times to clear it. He obtains the information this way but isn't sure he'll be able to retain it.

He moves on to the other temporary exhibition which is devoted to Modigliani, a name Robert doesn't know how to pronounce. He is not impressed. Modigliani's output seems to be mostly paintings of people with ridiculously long noses and naked women with big tits who like to show off their pubic hair. Robert would like to look more closely but feels embarrassed. The only other person in the room is a sour-faced gallery assistant, presumably guarding the paintings. No chance of getting past her. Anyway, he can't believe anyone would want to have such ugly and lopsided pictures hanging in their home. He's seen enough art for one day and heads for the area beyond the shop, hoping to find a rear exit.

There's a corridor to the left of the gents' loos which looks promising. Only problem is the sign above the entrance says PRIVATE NO ENTRY. It's a large sign so Robert can't pretend he hasn't noticed it. If he steps inside the corridor he'll be trespassing. His palms begin to itch. Come on Robert you can do this!

Every year Robert's school organised an outing to the seaside and every year Robert and his mum signed up to go. While his mum sat on the beach on her inflatable cushion eating scrambled egg butties and watching the other children play volleyball and bury one another up to their necks in sand, Robert waded out into the breakers. The drag of water on his thighs increased with every step but he kept on wading until he reached the point where only the tips of his toes were touching the sand, providing barely enough purchase to propel him back to shore. And every year he promised himself next time he'd go a bit further, until he was properly out of his depth so he had no choice but to swim. But he never did. Now, all these years later, he has the chance to take that extra step and prove he's not a coward.

A couple, laden with enough purchases to supply all the family birthdays for the next twelve months, come out of the shop and glance at Robert curiously. He waits till they are out of sight then, humming the *Mission Impossible* theme tune under his breath, he steps into the dimly lit corridor.

The clinking of china, the sizzling of hot oil and the gurgling of a coffee machine come from the cafe kitchen on the right. Robert takes the left-hand passage and soon reaches what appears to be a stockroom; at least the shelves are piled high with things they sell in the shop. The air in here is stuffy and the door handle is stiff but it will make a good hiding place if Robert needs one. A little further on he discovers two large built-in cupboards. He's about to investigate when he hears footsteps.

Bollocks! It's one of the waitresses – pale eyes, pasty complexion, good legs – and she's coming down the corridor towards him. Robert's knees turn weak and wobbly, and his heart thumps in his chest, working overtime. What's he supposed to do? He should have planned for a situation like this, thought up some excuse in advance. They say attack is the best defence. Robert walks towards the waitress, wearing what he hopes is an anxious expression.

'Can you help me please?'

'This area is private. You shouldn't be in here.'

'I know that but I'm looking for my son.'

'What makes you think he's in here?'

'I've looked everywhere else. He went to find a toilet and he hasn't come back.'

'And you've checked the toilets?'

'All of them. Twice. No sign of him.'

'How old is your son?'

Steady now. They'll send out a search party for a missing child if he's not careful. 'Sixteen. It was his birthday last week.'

She's puzzled.

'He's not all there,' Robert explains, tapping his head. 'One sandwich short of a picnic. Wanders off on his own then can't find the way back.'

'I can have a look if you like but—'

'Hang on a minute.' Robert pulls his mobile from his pocket in a gesture worthy of any soap. Dramatic pause while he reads an imaginary text. 'It's my wife. Panic over. The lad wasn't feeling well so she's taken him home.' He smiles, hoping he's done enough to convince the waitress he's genuine.

Robert is well chuffed at the way he handled that, thinking on his feet, not allowing himself to panic. Ten minutes ago he was a childless bachelor now he's acquired a wife and a grown-up son!

'Sorry to be a nuisance.'

The waitress smiles. 'No problem. I'm really pleased he's okay.'

Robert thanks her for her kindness. She has a nice face and he would like to stay and talk some more but he has an appointment with Samuel Baker on level two.

* * *

34

Will –	*Child alert!*
Bess –	*Gender?*
Will –	*Female.*
Bess –	*Age?*
Will –	*Seven or eight.*
Bess –	*Accompanied or solo?*
Will –	*Accompanied.*
Bess –	*Risk level?*
Will –	*Low.*
Bess –	*Are you sure? She could easily duck under the barrier and touch your canvas with her dirty fingers or stick chewing gum on your frame.*
Will –	*I don't think she'd want to. She's not interested in us. She doesn't appear to be interested in anything.*
Amy –	*She's not happy, that's for sure.*
Will –	*Never fear! Douglas will cheer her up.*

As they enter the Portrait Room Tia has the uncanny feeling they're interrupting a conversation in full flow, intruding on someone else's space. Faces emerge from the gloom and gradually come into focus. Everywhere eyes weigh them up, examining them as a student might examine a work of art. They come to a halt in front of a magnificent floor-to-ceiling painting of King George III. His costume is decorated with ribbons, silver buttons, tassels, frills and fringes. His head is turned upwards and slightly to the left, away from the viewer, as if he's looking down his nose at them. An expression typical of the privileged male in Tia's experience.

The only thing Tia can remember about George III is that he went mad and she's not even sure she's got the right George. If the painting had been of an Indian ruler – Emperor Ashok or Tipu Sultan or Jawaharlal Nehru – Tia could have filled in the background and answered Bindu's questions no problem. Though she has a feeling what her parents taught her about these heroes could be dismissed as folklore rather than history.

'He looks pretty miserable,' Tia says. 'I guess it's not much fun being king.'

'You would look miserable if you were in his position!'

Who said that?

Tia turns sharply to see a smartly dressed, silver-haired gentleman walking towards them, an identification badge on a lanyard hangs round his neck. Straight-backed and slim, with finely wrought features, he wouldn't look out of place in a life insurance advert. Douglas! He joined the gallery around the time Tia moved to archives and is responsible for leading guided tours and arranging seminars and workshops. He has a reputation for being one of the director's inner circle. Tia has spoken to him a couple of times when they shared the same break-out room during training but apart from that their paths haven't crossed.

'Welcome, young lady!' Douglas stoops to Bindu's height. 'It's not often we see a child in the Portrait Room. Most of them give up before they get this far.' He reaches out to shake her hand but Bindu conceals herself in the folds of Tia's coat.

Douglas turns to Tia. 'I know you work for Lucy but I'm ashamed to say I've forgotten your name.'

'That's okay. I wouldn't have known yours if you weren't wearing your badge.' It's a lie but it might make him feel better. Tia unravels Bindu and pushes her forward. 'This is Bindu. And I'm Tia.'

Tia, parrot. Her father gave her the name because the noise she made when she emerged from her mother's womb sounded to him more like a parrot's squawk than a baby's cry. You could say she's been squawking ever since! She squawked if she was hungry, or too hot or wanted to be bathed or just wanted to be the centre of attention. Her father thought she had the makings of a headmistress because when she squawked commands at her brother and sisters, they tended to obey. So he enrolled her in an English-medium school where she squawked at classmates and sometimes at her teachers which got her into trouble. She squawked because they couldn't see the best way to get things done whereas to Tia it was obvious.

Douglas looks at Bindu very seriously. 'Your mother thinks King George here is miserable. What's your opinion?'

'Thakuma.'

'Pardon?'

'She's not my mummy she's my Thakuma.'

'Grandmother,' Tia explains. 'I'm Bindu's grandmother. I'm looking after her during half-term.'

'You don't look old enough to be anyone's grandmother!'

Flattery obviously, all the same Tia finds it gratifying.

Douglas points to George III's portrait. 'Let me explain why I said you would look miserable if you were in George's position. The picture was painted in 1792. The ordinary citizens of France had just got rid of their king and queen. They thought they could rule their country by themselves.'

'Madame Guillotine.' Tia is pleased with herself for remembering. 'They cut off the heads of Louis XVI and Marie Antoinette and all the French aristocrats.'

Bindu curls her lips as if there is a bad smell. 'Cut off their heads? Ugh!'

Douglas reassures her it was all a long time ago and that it doesn't happen anymore.

Tia raises her eyebrows.

'Not in this country, at least,' Douglas concedes. 'You can see why George and all the other kings and queens in Europe were worried. They were afraid the same thing would happen to them.'

Bindu says, 'George looks silly. He's wearing tights and ladies' shoes.'

Tia is mortified. She is in favour of Bindu joining the conversation but there is no call to be rude. Douglas however doesn't seem to have a problem with Bindu's comments. In fact he encourages her!

'You're right! George would look silly if he walked around like that today but two hundred years ago that's what men wore. Fashions change, although much more slowly in those days than they do now.'

Douglas points at a picture hanging not far off. 'Meet Sir William Craven. He was born exactly one hundred years before George. Can you see William's wig is longer than George's? And he has a lacy bow tied round his neck.'

Bindu nods. Douglas has her full attention now.

'Let's see what you think of the ladies.' He strides over to a picture of a woman dressed in a heavy, richly embroidered costume, dripping with pearls and precious jewels, and a wide, stiff ruff at her neck. Tia and Bindu follow.

'Here we have Elizabeth Countess of Shrewsbury better known as Bess of Hardwick. Isn't she splendid? She was born one hundred years before William. Bess had four husbands and more money than anyone else in England after the queen!'

'Why did she need four husbands?' Bindu looks puzzled.

'Not all at the same time!' Douglas laughs. 'When one husband died she married another one.' He turns to the painting hanging beside Bess. 'And this is Amy Robsart. Her dress is a lovely shade of green, don't you think? But it must have been very uncomfortable to wear. The ruff reminds me of a frill-necked lizard!'

While Bindu is admiring Amy's dress, Douglas and Tia move a little further down the room and stop in front of a painting of a woman wearing a haggard expression. Her gorgeous golden dress is crumpled and two worried-looking men peep at her from behind her chair.

'Behold the Virgin Queen, Gloriana, Elizabeth I herself!'

'Is that really supposed to be Elizabeth?' Tia looks doubtful. 'She looks very different from other pictures I've seen of her.'

'She's just given orders to cut off Mary Queen of Scots' head.' He drops his voice. 'So insensitive of the curator to hang Amy and Queen Elizabeth side by side.'

Tia asks him to explain.

'Queen Elizabeth was overfond of Robert Dudley, Amy's husband. She insisted he stay at court and wouldn't let him out of her sight.'

'Poor Amy!'

'Poor Amy indeed. She was dead within the year. Pushed down the stairs or poisoned, depending on how you interpret the evidence.'

Tia marvels at Douglas's enthusiasm. He could be talking about something that happened to his own family only yesterday.

'I'm sorry. I can go on like this forever. I expect you've had enough of me.'

'Not at all. Please don't stop. It's so much more fun with your commentary.'

'Well, if you are sure…'

He moves from one picture to another supplying background detail and bringing the subjects to life. His enthusiasm is infectious; Bindu wanders round the room on her own taking time to study each picture until she comes to the portrait of a girl a few years older than she is.

'Thakuma! Come and see this one. Isn't she lovely?'

Tia crosses the room to take a look. The canvas is coarse and hasn't absorbed the paint evenly, more like a sketch than a finished work of art, and yet the fragile picture is heartbreakingly beautiful. The girl's face is partially obscured by deep shadows. The narrow chin, the full lips, the deeply expressive eyes are painted with the lightest touch. A tear trembles on the girl's lashes, and shyness colours her cheeks a delicate pink. Her simple dress is in stark contrast to the elaborate costumes and jewellery worn by her neighbours. No frills, no headdress, no ornaments, only a gossamer shawl resting lightly on her bare shoulder. The picture is soft focus, slightly muzzy, as if the girl's tears have brought tears to the eyes of the viewer.

'Ah! You've fallen under Hedova's spell.' Douglas joins them. 'We're all a little bit in love with Hedova.'

'Hedova? That's an unusual name.'

'The title of the painting is *Head of a Girl*. We call her Hedova for short, out of affection. They're not certain who she is or when she lived or who painted her.'

'Is that why she's so sad?' Bindu asks. 'I'd be sad if I didn't have a mummy.'

Tia doesn't know what all the fuss is about. In her opinion the girl in the portrait looks pathetic and spineless, a weak character weighed down by self-pity.

They'll have to go soon. Tia promised to give Bindu a hot meal before Subir comes to pick her up. Bindu doesn't want to leave, she'd happily sit and look at Hedova all evening. When Tia insists, Bindu asks if she can take a photo of the painting so she can show her parents. Douglas points to the No Photography sign.

'But that man was taking photos!' Bindu wails. 'Why can't we?'

'Which man?' Tia looks around.

'The man who came in while you and Douglas uncle were talking.'

'I didn't see anyone.'

'Well I did and he was taking photos with his mobile. Why don't you believe me, Thakuma? You never believe what I say.'

Douglas says he didn't see anyone either. Tia is on the point of telling Bindu she must have imagined it, when Douglas, with infuriating honesty, adds, 'We didn't see him but that doesn't mean he wasn't here.'

Douglas insists on accompanying them downstairs and into the foyer where Tia thanks him for entertaining them. 'My pleasure. Such an appreciative audience! Come again and we can look in the other rooms. In fact you could come back on Wednesday if you're free. I'm leading a tour of the permanent collections. I try to cater for all ages during the school holidays. I think you'd both enjoy it.'

Bindu jumps up and down a few inches from Tia's face. 'Say yes. Please say yes!'

Tia pushes her away, laughing, and promises they'll come if they can.

Evie waits till Douglas is out of earshot. 'He's a really nice guy.'

'I agree.'

'And good with children.'

'Very.' Tia takes Bindu's hand.

'And about the right age.'

'We have to go.'

Evie grins. 'See you Wednesday!'

As they drive home Bindu tells Tia the joke she's just made up.

'Knock, knock.'

'Who's there?'

'Douglas.'

'Douglas who?'

'Dug less holes!'

'Fewer holes,' Tia corrects her. 'You can't say *less* holes. It has to be *fewer*.'

She catches sight of Bindu's face in the mirror. 'But that doesn't matter in this case because it's a joke. You can say what you like when you're telling a joke.'

Will –	*Dougie was on top form today.*
Bess –	*It's what he does best, perform in front of an audience. Especially a female audience. Do you think he's hoping to impress the grandmother?*
Will –	*He certainly impressed the child!*
Bess –	*The way to a woman's heart is through her children or in this case grandchildren.*

Amy –   *You're so cynical. Douglas saw the little one needed cheering up and he did what was required. He loves children. So do I.*

Elizabeth – *Here we go! She died childless and she blames me for it. She forgets that I had to forgo the delights of family life for the sake of my country, though kings and emperors and princes across Europe were falling over each other in their eagerness to be my husband.*

Bess –   *Children are a mixed blessing. I remember George telling us his darling daughter Amelia, his favourite, fell for an equerry and died of a broken heart when Queen Charlotte refused to allow them to marry.*

Will –   *Talking of broken hearts, I've often wondered if that's why our dear little Hedova is so sad. Perhaps her parents didn't approve of her choice of husband.*

Siegfried – *No! That's impossible. I am her first and her last. She loves me.*

Bess –   *And how do you know that? She doesn't speak.*

Siegfried – *She speaks to me with her eyes.*

Bess –   *And will you kindly tell us what her eyes say?*

Will –   *Don't tease the lad! Tell me Siegfried, if you and Hedova love each other why is she so sad?*

Siegfried – *Because we can't be together. I have to keep fighting that wretched bird and my darling has to sit and watch.*

Bess –   *She is much too young to be giving her heart to anyone. These childhood romances never last. I married for love at the age of fifteen and was widowed two years later.*

Will –   *In my opinion she's suffering from an identity crisis. Can you imagine not knowing who you are?*

Bess –   *Perhaps she's a witch, or the daughter of a witch. There is something unreal, a ghostly quality about her.*

Will –   *Maybe that's why her neck is invisible, because it bears the imprint of Satan's teeth. In my time the whole world was on the lookout for witches.*

Bess –   *I think Bindu (I've never come across that name before) understood Hedova's sadness. Did you see the way they looked at each other?*

Will –   *I heard Bindu say she would like to have Hedova as her sister. There is a certain similarity in appearance and demeanour, don't you think?*

Siegfried – *Hedova is way more beautiful!*

Bess –   *What did you make of that man taking photographs? I didn't like the look of him. I'd send my men to spy on him if I had the wherewithal.*

Will –   *He remains innocent until proven guilty. A principle first formulated during George's reign as it happens though the concept goes back to ancient times. I'm surprised Douglas didn't spot him. He's usually pretty quick to investigate anything out of the ordinary.*

Bess –   *Like I said, he was preoccupied with the grandmother. We'll be seeing more of her, I bet my frame on it.*

CHAPTER TWO

It's day two of his new life and so far Robert is thoroughly enjoying it. Exploring the private corridor, checking out the alarms, photographing Samuel's portrait and working out where the back entrance was; at any point someone could have challenged him and asked him to explain himself. Like when you're tobogganing down the slope and suddenly realise you're heading straight for a tree. It's impossible to think clearly, you have to rely on instinct, and for a few moments things could go either way. It's the not knowing that makes it exciting. For years he's followed the easy path and played safe. Now he's into risk-taking big time. He honestly doesn't know how this robbery will pan out. That's what makes it exciting, that's why he's doing it.

Robert was up before six this morning. Now it's seven and he's flipping through the pages of the tabloids in the newsagent's over the road from the Whitler Gallery. He's here because it's a good lookout point for keeping tabs on the early morning comings and goings of the staff. With any luck he'll find a weak spot, a particular time in the day when they become careless and let security slip.

From his inspection yesterday Robert has established there are no alarms on the individual pictures which is a relief, and he has a pretty clear idea of where the CCTV cameras are. The best way to deal with them is to cover the lenses with a piece of cloth, which sounds straightforward but they're beyond his reach so he needs to practise throwing accurately from below.

Seven thirty. Who's this? A middle-aged woman wheels her bike through the staff car park and round the back of the building. She must be the caretaker. A few minutes later the lights go on in the reception area and then in one of the windows in the staff block. Robert waits to see if the stairwell lights up, which would mean the caretaker is checking the upstairs galleries. No. The stairs and upper rooms remain dark.

'You going to buy that?' The young woman behind the counter nods at the newspaper in Robert's hand. 'We're not a bleeding library!'

Snotty little madam. Robert replaces the paper and walks a little further down the pavement till he finds a café catering for the 'didn't have time for breakfast' trade. He chooses a table with a good view of the gallery.

Eight o'clock. A couple of cars drive into the staff car park. A little later the lights go on in the café.

'Are you ready to order?' Robert is so intent on looking out of the window, the waitress has to repeat the question.

'Sorry. Pot of tea and a toasted tea cake. Lightly done. Two jams no butter.'

He settles down to watch. One by one six more cars arrive and by eight thirty the lights are on in most of the offices. So there is a window of opportunity, as they say, between seven thirty and eight, after the caretaker has disarmed the alarm but before any other staff arrive. Half an hour when it's possible to steal the painting. There may be other opportunities during the day but they're unlikely to be as good as this. Robert will either have to sleep overnight in the building so he's ready to start as soon as the caretaker arrives next day, or follow the caretaker in at seven thirty without being seen. Either way, with any luck the theft won't be discovered until the doors open to the public at ten and he and the picture should be well away by then.

Robert pays the bill and sets off for home via the market where he plans to buy a pair of knitted gloves, not too thick or he won't be able to feel what he's doing, and a pair of ladies' tights. The gloves aren't a problem but the tights prove more complicated.

'What kind of tights?' the stallholder enquires. Seeing Robert bewildered, she outlines the choices. 'Ten, twenty or forty denier. Plain or patterned. With gusset or without.'

He isn't much clearer. 'Could you give me some advice?'

'Happy to. For starters who are you buying them for?'

'My sister.' Robert adds to his rapidly expanding family. 'She's broken her leg and can't leave the house.'

The stallholder looks puzzled. 'Then she'll not be wearing tights for a good while, they won't fit over the plaster. Unless she's planning to cut off one of the legs. I've heard some of them do that.'

She sorts through the pile and picks out a thick pair with a pretty pattern. 'These will keep her warm but they don't have a gusset. And these here have a gusset but they're plain.' Robert takes both pairs, stretches them taut and holds them up to the light.

'What's the difference? I mean why would somebody want to have a gusset?' He immediately regrets the question.

'You've got me there.' The stallholder shouts over to another stall. 'Can you help us out? This young man wants to know what's the advantage of a gusset.'

Every single person in the entire market stops what they're doing to listen to the reply, or so it seems to Robert.

'You don't need to wear knickers if your tights have a gusset.'

The stallholder turns back to Robert. 'Did you hear that? Does your sister wear knickers under her tights?'

Sweating with embarrassment, Robert chooses a pair and makes his escape.

He rehearses his plan as he walks. The tricky bit is how to move the picture away from the staff car park without being seen, and do it quickly. The car park is completely cut off from the surrounding streets, by a hedge on one side and iron railings on the other two sides. He can slide the picture between the iron bars and then come round the other side to collect it but how will he know if the coast is clear? Somebody could be walking past at that very moment and wonder what on earth is going on when a large picture suddenly emerges from the hedge and blocks their path! The best option would be a getaway vehicle driven by an assistant waiting for him at the back of the building. But Robert doesn't want an assistant meddling with his plans. He wants to keep the ransom money for himself.

Robert hasn't yet decided where to hide the picture, bearing in mind he may have to leave it there quite a while if the negotiations for payment of a ransom drag on. It needs to be a remote place where no one goes and no one would think of hiding a picture. He does have one idea. There's a disused graveyard on South Road. If he can find a way to conceal the picture it could lie there undisturbed for a week or two while they come to an agreement on the ransom. That's a point, how much is he going to ask – no, how much will he *demand*? He's the one calling the shots. Ten thousand, fifteen? He comes over all goosebumps at the thought of so much cash for so little outlay.

He has to step aside to avoid a group of punters taking a smoking break outside William Hill. They peer nervously at their watches, screwing up their eyes against the cigarette smoke. One is celebrating a win. He's jiggling with excitement up and down the pavement, balancing heel to toe along the kerb and waving his arms. Someone opens the door of the betting shop and shouts, 'Two thirty Sedgefield.' The punters pinch off the ends of their roll-ups and dive back inside.

Hard to believe but Robert has never been inside a bookies, let alone laid a bet. His mum couldn't stop her husband throwing money away on the horses but she was determined to stop her son. She made Robert put one hand on the Highway Code (because she once heard someone describe it as The Drivers' Bible) and swear he'd never go into a bookies.

'You could try looking where you're going.' An elderly woman heavily laden with shopping bags blocks his path.

'Sorry. Thinking about something else.'

'Tell that to the bus driver. "Sorry" won't do you much good when you're under his bus!'

Her remark brings Robert up short. She's right! Who knows how long he'll be around to enjoy the fruits of his labour? He has everything in place, he's all ready to go, why wait? Why not do it tonight?

* * *

Tia presses her palms together in *Namaskar*, then arching her back moves into the satisfying stretch of the extended mountain pose. Forward fold next, grasping her ankles and tucking her head in, followed by a lunge with right leg extended behind her and head thrown back. She sends the left leg to join the right as she stiffens her back for the plank, holds it a while, then drops down onto her stomach with upper body raised in cobra. Straining to keep her knees locked, she moves shakily into the downwards-facing dog. Another lunge, left leg this time, another forward fold and back up to the mountain pose. Palms pressed in a final *Namaskar,* she brings the sequence to a close. Tia repeats the cycle three more times, then rolls up her yoga mat and tucks it away behind the sofa.

She has been performing *Surya Namaskar* each morning since her mother introduced her to the sequence when she was fifteen. She still finds the exercise a source of comfort and strength. It's only because she's disciplined herself to daily practice in front of a full-length mirror to check for faults, that her aging body can still perform the moves. In her opinion there's no point in doing yoga or any other form of exercise half-heartedly, you have to be committed if you want results. Her yoga class is well attended but no one approaches the sessions as seriously as she does. It's a common problem, Tia finds, this lack of self-discipline and commitment. There's a constant stream of new people signing up but they don't stick at it, most of them give up as soon as it begins to hurt.

Carrying her glass of fresh mango juice into the conservatory, Tia looks out over the wet and bedraggled garden. It's crying out for attention but it will have to wait until half-term is over – unless she can persuade Bindu to help? Highly improbable! No! It's not fair to blame Bindu's half-term for the state of her garden. She has been finding it difficult to keep on top of the weeding and mowing and planting and cutting back for some time. She really must sort out a gardener.

People regularly flatter her, saying she doesn't look old enough to be a granny. What nonsense! She's put on a kilo this year and has lost so much hair she's been forced to have what's left cut short, so that it spreads out and gives the impression of volume. She has to touch up the roots every fortnight rather than once a month, now that they have all turned grey. Fortunately Tia has inherited her mother's firm jawline and prominent cheek bones so that even if she shaved her head she would still be beautiful.

Her mental powers are diminishing, though she would deny it if challenged. Nor would she admit to occasionally nodding off after lunch. It's quite an effort each morning to conjure up the bright and purposeful expression which is her hallmark, and even more of an effort to sustain it. The sparkling energy and spirit of enquiry which have accompanied Tia throughout her life are beginning to fade and at times she just can't be bothered.

Bindu however appears to be moving in the opposite direction, from lethargy to liveliness, if Subir's phone call last night is anything to go by.

'What have you done to her, Ma? She won't stay in bed. Too excited. Can't stop talking about Hedova, the girl in the painting she saw in the Whitler Gallery. Hedova – what kind of a name is that? Bindu's adamant she's going to see the picture again. She mentioned someone called Douglas too. He's made a big impression. What have you been up to?'

Good question. Tia mulls it over. What was it that caused the transformation in Bindu's behaviour yesterday? It can't just be down to the fact she was surrounded by stimulating works of art. She'd been her normal moody self until Douglas appeared. No, it was definitely something about Douglas. His enthusiasm perhaps? And the way he brings the pictures alive with his comments. Makes you see things in the paintings you never would have seen on your own. Well, Tia can do that too if she has enough time to prepare. Truth is, she is a little bit jealous of Douglas, or rather of Bindu's relationship with Douglas. And for that reason, she's not taking Bindu anywhere near the Whitler Gallery today.

'I looked it up,' Subir says when he drops Bindu off, a mere twenty minutes later than agreed.

'Looked what up?'

'The painting, *Head of a Girl*. Bindu wanted me to print off a copy of the picture so she could put it on her bedroom wall. Wouldn't give me any peace until I did. She's brought it with her to show you.'

Bindu holds up a laminated copy of Hedova. Tia studies the *please feel sorry for me* face peeking out from the shadows. Was it a real girl with a genuine reason to be sad, in which case what was the reason? Or a model who has been instructed to adopt this expression? Or was she a figment of the artist's imagination, a generic face to practise on? When Subir leaves, Bindu barely says goodbye she is so engrossed in her picture of Hedova.

'Come on then young lady, we don't want to be late,' Tia chivvies Bindu affectionately.

'Late for what? I didn't know we were going out.'

Tia explains they are going to a young people's theatre workshop, a whole day programme based on the university campus. Parents and guardians are also invited. The event is to be led by a well-known TV presenter, and professional actors will demonstrate their skills in a variety of workshops. Bindu throws herself onto the sofa and buries her head in the cushions.

'I don't want to go.'

'I think it sounds really good. I'm looking forward to seeing what these celebrities look like face to face.'

'I don't care what they look like. I don't like acting and I don't like the theatre.'

'I already bought the tickets.'

'I never said I wanted to go. Why didn't you ask me first, before you bought the tickets?' Bindu's voice is muffled by the upholstery.

Tia doesn't know what to say. She is being held to account by her seven-year-old granddaughter and because Bindu's parents champion her right to choose, Tia can't tell her that she'll jolly well do as she's told.

'We'll go this morning and see what it's like. If you don't want to stay for the afternoon session that's okay, we'll come straight home.'

When they arrive at the venue Bindu refuses to get out of the car. Tia resorts to threats – if Bindu doesn't join the workshop this morning then tomorrow she can't go to the Whitler for Douglas's guided tour. This has the desired effect but only briefly; for her next trick Bindu refuses to take off her padded jacket despite the room being very warm. And so it goes on; she won't introduce herself, she won't read the part assigned to her or try on costumes or help design and make the scenery – all on the pretext of being overcome by shyness. By midday Tia is only too glad to leave the workshop and bring Bindu home.

After a bad-tempered lunch (Bindu chooses to miss out the savoury course and go straight to the ice cream – as if!) Tia suggests they do some baking. She tries to involve Bindu in every aspect of the task from choosing a recipe and weighing the ingredients to spooning the mixture into the paper cases. But Bindu quickly loses focus and has to be constantly chivvied. She's not even interested in sampling what they bake.

While they wait for Subir to arrive, Bindu takes out her picture of Hedova and presses it against her cheek. 'I'll see you tomorrow,' she whispers.

'You will make sure your daddy isn't late, won't you? The tour begins at ten.'

Tia is looking forward to the tour almost as much as Bindu is. Apart from being a good presenter, Douglas is the perfect example of an old-fashioned English gentleman. The kind of man who holds the car door open for you to climb in and pulls your chair out as you go to sit down, and asks your permission before removing his jacket at dinner and collects your coat when you're ready to leave and helps you put it on. The kind of man who makes you feel like a lady. She's pretty sure Shompa would say that's sexist but to be honest Tia doesn't care.

She is accustomed to Indian men who don't have a clue about the meaning of 'ladies and children first', who in a shipwreck would be first into the lifeboats because they have been brought up to think they are infinitely more valuable than their female counterparts. Men who say please, sorry and thank you not because they mean it but simply to conform to the habits of their adopted country. Douglas couldn't be more different; why wouldn't she be looking forward to seeing him again?

Later that evening Tia opens her laptop and searches for *Head of a Girl*. It's a common title; she finds pictures listed under the same name by Leonardo, Renoir, Picasso, Lucian Freud and Jean Baptiste Greuze... Ah! She recognises that name. Greuze is the artist who, according to Douglas, used to be credited with painting Hedova. She looks at other pictures by Greuze and can't see any similarities. His girls are plump and have waxy complexions. Their expressions are cheerful and confident, in fact just the kind of child she wishes Bindu was, but completely the opposite of Hedova.

Modern scholars attribute Hedova to Francesco Furini or one of his pupils. It's true most of Furini's subjects look troubled like Hedova, anguished even, but unlike her their bodies are robust and solid. If you tried to touch Hedova your hand would pass right through her like a ghost. One scholar thinks Furini's painting *Poetry* has echoes of *Head of a Girl* but Tia can't see it herself. The model for *Poetry* has passion and purpose, Hedova is simply pathetic. In all probability they will never know who painted her or who she is. Strange that she has lived in the limelight for three hundred years, while her contemporaries are completely forgotten.

* * *

Having decided there's no point putting the burglary off any longer, Robert has no time to waste. He hurries home, dumps his bag just inside the front door and pops down to Jamie's flat. Zelda, one of the other tenants, on her way back from the mailroom wonders what a young student and a middle-aged bachelor have in common.

'Hi there. What can I do for you?' Jamie has the glazed eyes of someone who has been staring too long at a screen.

'Are you on your own?'

'Yep, unfortunately. Entirely alone.' Jamie throws the door wide open. 'Come in.'

Robert chooses a kitchen chair rather than the sofa, less likely to harbour germs. 'I've got a favour to ask. My uncle just died and left me an antique mirror. One of those large ones with a fancy frame. It's a bit worse for wear but it'll look okay when it's been restored. I've found just the right person to do it. She's based on South Road, opposite the cemetery, but I don't have any way of getting the mirror up there. Is there any chance we could use your car?'

'No problem. If the mirror doesn't fit in the boot we can put it on the back seat. When are you thinking of?'

'Tomorrow morning. Early. Soon after eight.'

'Sorry. I've scheduled a tutorial for eight thirty. It's reading week but my tutor is superkeen. I could do it after twelve.'

'That won't work. The house has to be cleared by half eight. Any chance you could change the time of your tutorial, just this once?' Robert doesn't like putting on the pressure but there's no other way.

'I suppose I could try.'

Jamie calls his tutor who agrees to reschedule the appointment.

Robert gets to his feet. 'Really appreciate it. I'll be waiting for you on Whitler Avenue, that's the lane running behind the gallery, soon after eight.' He slaps Jamie on the back. 'I owe you.'

Who knew Robert could duck and dive so skilfully? He's now added an uncle to his list of family members, not to mention appointing an assistant without having to share the profits!

Back in his flat Robert removes the tights from their packaging. Wearing them over your head is supposed to distort the features, making you unrecognisable. He puts his head into the upper section so that the gusset sits on his crown like a Jewish *kippah* and the legs hang down on either side like enormous spaniel ears. It's too loose. He pulls the tights down further, so that his head is pushed up into one of the legs. That's a better fit but he realises now the material is so thick that, even when it's fully stretched, he can't see through it.

He fetches a pair of scissors and cuts one leg free as per the stallholder's unwitting recommendation. Then he cuts two eyeholes but when he puts the leg back over his head he can't align the holes with his eyes. He pulls it off and cuts the holes wider. Now the holes sit comfortably over his ears but he still can't see a thing. Sod it! He chucks the mutilated tights in the bin. What's wrong with a balaclava anyway?

Robert fetches the holdall he bought for the gym but has never used, and places it on the table ready for packing. Now concentrate, what does he need? Four hand towels –

make that five in case he miscounted – screwdrivers, chisel, gloves, his balaclava, a bedsheet and some string. As he collects the items one by one and places them in the bag, the reality of what he is about to do strikes home. His palms begin to itch and he suffers waves of abdominal cramp. He has to sit down abruptly to avoid fainting. An attack of nerves, but there's no way he'll let them get the better of him.

The important thing is to keep remembering how exciting it is and not let himself imagine what will happen if he gets caught. What is it the Yanks say? 'Nothing to fear but fear itself.' Nothing is going to go wrong but if it does, well then at least he will have proved he's not a coward.

He needs to rest. He won't get much sleep, holed up in that stuffy stockroom. Robert zaps through the television channels. It's the usual diet of cookery – the chef runs out of superlatives to describe the taste of the dish he has cooked; antiques – the expert waxes lyrical about the superb quality and provenance of a piece of art deco pottery; or property – the featured couple exclaim in delight as they realise they can buy a country mansion for the price of their one-bedroom London flat. At three fifteen Robert turns off the telly and rechecks the contents of his holdall.

For a moment he wonders whether to pack a toothbrush, shaver and a change of underwear but quickly dismisses the idea as ridiculous!

Standing in front of the mirror he puts on a pair of zero-power spectacles and assesses the effect. He doesn't look much different but some people might be fooled. He adds a baseball cap turned back to front and one of his dad's scarves. Yes, that does the trick. If he's unlucky and the cameras catch him, he won't be easily recognised. At half past three he leaves the flat and sets off for the Whitler Gallery with his head held high and a new-found confidence fuelling his every step.

There's a light drizzle and the cold, damp air blows straight into his lungs. The whole city centre has been transformed into a rabbit warren with workmen tearing up tarmac and felling trees on all sides. It's difficult to make any sense of the alterations unless you've studied the plans drawn up by the city architects, which Robert hasn't. He doesn't object to change if the changes are for the better but he is sorry to see the cutting down of trees and demolition of buildings he's known since he was a child.

He reaches the Whitler just as the afternoon workshops are coming to an end. Everywhere children and parents are collecting their stuff and preparing to leave and saying their goodbyes. Unnoticed in the general kerfuffle, Robert skirts round the edge of the foyer trying to keep clear of the sight lines of the CCTV cameras.

The layout looks different today. Where is the entrance to the staff section to the rear of the building? Robert feels the sweat trickling cold down his back. He returns to his starting point. Last time he reached the corridor via the toilets. He follows the Toilets sign and immediately sees the entrance to the corridor. Having checked the coast is clear he steps into the corridor. He locates the stockroom and slips inside, leaving the door open just a fraction. To his horror the light comes on, triggered by his movement. He hadn't thought of that. He must find a hiding place quickly and then keep absolutely still. He squeezes into the gap between two tall steel filing cabinets, pulls the holdall in after him and waits. The floor between the cabinets is thick with dust and tangles of hair and cobwebs, as if the cleaner deposits the contents of her dustpan there instead of emptying it in the bin. Robert hopes the dust won't make him sneeze.

After what seems like half an hour but is probably only a few minutes the light switches itself off and he gradually eases his limbs into a more a comfortable position. He's struck by how quiet it is, almost peaceful. Only the occasional muffled voice, the distant banging of a door and the revving of an engine break the silence. He shifts position again, very cautiously so as not to trigger the light. The gallery closes its doors at five. He doesn't know what happens after that; no doubt the caretaker does a round of the building before locking up. If he's really unlucky the cleaners will arrive.

Robert can barely see his watch now; once the light is switched off he'll be in complete darkness and his torch is in the bottom of his holdall, difficult to reach. How will he know what time it is? Of course, stupid, his mobile! Which reminds him… hampered by the confined space he struggles to pull his phone from his pocket and switches it to silent.

It's kind of comforting pressed up against two solid objects. Robert barely slept a wink the previous night and it's not long before he dozes off. He's jolted awake sometime later by the sound of footsteps coming down the corridor. The caretaker doing her final rounds most likely. The footsteps come to a halt outside the stockroom. He holds his breath. He can hear the swoosh, swoosh of blood passing behind his eardrums as it pumps round his body.

What will he do if the caretaker pushes the door wide open and sees him? More to the point what will he do if the caretaker catches hold of him? She's a heavily built, muscular sort of woman and Robert has a feeling he might not get away from her that easily. What would he actually do – punch her in the face, crack her skull with the chisel, stab her in the ribs with the screwdriver? When it comes down to the gory details Robert can feel his tongue dry up and his face turn grey. The door closes and the footsteps retreat leaving him in complete darkness and shaking with relief.

There follows the most terrible night Robert has ever spent. The central heating goes off around six and the temperature in the stockroom drops rapidly. He shivers spasmodically and every muscle in his body aches. He hasn't eaten since Tuesday lunchtime and is dying of hunger and thirst. He's also desperate for the loo but can't do anything about it. He simply has to lie still and count off the hours until the morning and keep reminding himself that he's enjoying it.

CHAPTER THREE

As usual Douglas is awake by five. Even as a child he was a poor sleeper. According to his parents he would creep into their room at midnight asking them to read him a story. An hour later he was back complaining some of the jigsaw puzzle pieces were missing and soon after that he was asking for help with the Meccano tower he was building. Long before the birds began their dawn chorus, he was begging his father to unlock the front door so he could go and play in the garden. Douglas himself doesn't see it as a problem; he enjoys his sleep, it's just that he doesn't need as much of it as other people seem to. In his considered opinion we waste a great deal of time lying in bed when we could be up and doing.

He goes to the bathroom before performing a sequence of stretches and bends to the beat of a metronome, as prescribed by his physio. Satisfied he's given his aging muscles a good workout Douglas goes into the kitchen to prepare his morning cup of tea, a blend of Darjeeling and Assam, loose leaf not tea bags.

Today he's in a particularly cheerful mood. He knows there's a good reason he's feeling cheerful but he's damned if he can recall what it is! While he waits for the central heating to take the edge off the early morning chill, he racks his brain trying to remember. It has something to do with the guided tour he leads every Wednesday. Yes! That's it! Today Tia and her granddaughter Bindu are going to participate. What a delightful child. Sensitive, intelligent, pretty and not afraid to speak her mind. She immediately fell for Hedova. To pick out that particular painting from a room full of splendid portraits, quite remarkable! Although Douglas is not sure Tia would agree.

The sight of one solitary cup on the breakfast tray brings him up short. It's two years since Douglas buried his wife but still now his heart contracts at the sight of one solitary breakfast cup.

He buried his wife two years ago but she died many years before that. The medics call it Early Onset Dementia or EOD. She was only fifty when it struck and physically very fit. She resigned from her job in the registrar's office at the university and filled her days with walking, instead of sorting out bureaucratic messes. She walked from their house along the dual carriageway into the city centre and back perpetually, summer and winter, as if by continuous walking she could remain one step ahead of the disease.

She was known locally as the bag lady because when she walked, her hands clutched half a dozen carrier bags. She wore the same sweater and anorak in the sweltering heat of summer as she did in the middle of winter when roadside puddles were covered by a thick layer of ice. She lifted up her toes with each step and threw her feet out in front, as instructed by the physio, which gave her an unusual gait. Her head jiggled continuously as if it was stuck on the end of a wire spring.

Every morning Douglas prepared a breakfast of pancake and maple syrup and made sure she ate it before she left the house. He watched her move off, unsteady at first then picking up speed as she established a rhythm; and every morning he wondered if this would be the last time he saw her alive. So, when one afternoon a police car drew up in front of his house, Douglas guessed immediately why it had come.

The driver of the car didn't stand a chance, they said. He didn't see the woman with the bags until she stepped into the road. She didn't even turn her head to check for traffic, just stepped off the kerb straight in front of his car. She didn't suffer. The impact was enough to knock her unconscious and she died in the ambulance on the way to hospital. It wasn't Douglas's fault. His wife wanted to walk and he had no right to stop her.

At the inquest the expert witness said research shows that people with dementia know how to keep themselves safe on the roads as if by instinct or long-established habit. They might get hopelessly lost searching for houses and streets long since demolished and remodelled but it's very rare for them to cause a road traffic accident. It wasn't till after the cremation that Douglas realised the significance of the expert's testimony. The implication was that when his wife stepped into the road she knew exactly what she was doing. She would certainly be capable of such a brave act if she felt it was the best way out. And no doubt it was for her, but her death robbed Douglas's life of meaning and purpose. There have been times when he thought he couldn't go on.

One day, doing his best to keep the demons at bay, Douglas called into the Whitler Gallery and discovered the

Portrait Room. It soon became a regular habit. He spent many hours there offloading his sorrow onto Sir William Craven of Benham Valence and Coombe Abbey, and Elizabeth Countess of Shrewsbury, aka Bess of Hardwick. Will and Bess gazed at Douglas while he rehearsed the cruel details of his wife's illness for the umpteenth time, and sang her praises and wept. William's expression is sensitive and sympathetic with a touch of humour playing around the lips; he doesn't let the vagaries of life get him down. Bess is more worldly wise, there's nothing you can tell her she hasn't heard before, but Douglas senses real warmth and tenderness behind her penetrating gaze.

If you were looking for a rational explanation you could say that talking things through while looking at a human face helps him come to terms with his bereavement. But Douglas isn't wedded to rational explanations. All he knows is that he wouldn't have survived the last couple of years without Will and Bess and the Portrait Room.

About six months after his first visit, a vacancy arose at the gallery for a part-time educational liaison officer, a role Douglas felt qualified to perform with his teaching background. The timing couldn't have been better; if the opportunity had arisen any earlier he couldn't have coped. He applied and was successful, principally because he was already a familiar figure in the gallery and the director didn't see him as a threat to his authority, which is more than can be said for some of the candidates. And Douglas has never looked back.

* * *

Robert lies there, wedged between two steel cabinets, listening to the council house clock strike midnight then one then two o'clock. He drifts off into a fitful sleep and the next time he opens his eyes he has no sensation in his limbs. He wriggles his ankles and feels the blood flow back into his feet. He moves through his body flexing his muscles and moving each part as much as the confined space allows. The process is painful but reassuring. He needs to be ready for action the moment the caretaker arrives. He checks his mobile. Five o'clock. Another two and a half hours to wait! He no longer has the urge to urinate, as if his body has reabsorbed his piss. But he'd do anything for a hot drink. He drifts into a fitful snooze and dreams he's spending the night in a jungle stocked full of brown bears and python as a punishment for abseiling down the front of the council house.

A door slams. Someone flushes the toilet. Robert is wide awake. He's not in the jungle, he's in the Whitler Gallery. Someone else, presumably the caretaker, is in the building too so there's no need to worry about the alarm. On with the gloves and balaclava. He wriggles out from his hiding place, trying to move quickly in spite of his protesting joints. A sudden burst of light fills the room. He must get out as soon as possible. The door handle yields to his touch, thank God for that. He steps cautiously into the corridor. He can hear water running and the clink of a teaspoon against china. The caretaker is making her morning mug of tea.

Robert tiptoes back along the corridor and into the foyer. Here he pauses. Is he ready for this? Once he climbs those two flights of stairs his exit is blocked. There's nowhere to hide on level one or two. If they find him up there, he's done for. A burst of adrenaline propels him forward.

Concentrating on precisely where and how he places his feet, he creeps noiselessly up the grand staircase. The nerves have disappeared. He knows what he's got to do and he's totally focussed on doing it.

Bess –   *That's strange. Someone is coming upstairs.*
Will –   *I don't recognise the footsteps. They're very quiet.*
Bess –   *It's not the caretaker. She makes a lot of noise. Sometimes I think she does it deliberately.*
Will –   *Why would she do that?*
Bess –   *To let us know she's on her way; so she doesn't catch us doing something we shouldn't.*

Robert feels his way along the wall and into the Portrait Room where the only light comes from the emergency exit signs. He takes the towels from his bag and throws one up towards the spot where he thinks one of the cameras is. Sod it! The towel comes straight back down. He should have practised. He tries again and this time the towel catches and stays put. It's not until he's covered the fourth camera that it occurs to him it's so dark the CCTV footage will be useless as a means of identification. It's all been a bleeding waste of time! He goes back to the doorway and runs his hand up and down the wall feeling for the middle row, third picture from the left. Got it!

Robert locates the projecting flange and tries to insert his screwdriver into the head of one of the screws but fails because the grooves are clogged up, probably with paint. He tries to scrape them clean with his thumbnail but finally has to resort to gouging them out with the chisel. He can hear the caretaker rustling papers on the reception desk.

He holds his breath. The clock on the council house tower strikes eight times. Christ! This is taking much longer than it should. The staff will arrive any minute now.

Will –   *He's stopped in front of Hedova. Poor child.*
Siegfried – *No! No! Not Hedova. My darling, the light of my life! What is he doing now? I can't see from here.*
Will –   *He's loosening her screws.*
Siegfried – *Take me! Leave her alone and take me instead.*
Bess –   *He's taking out her screws.*
Siegfried – *NO!*
Bess –   *Poor child. She must be terrified.*

Supporting the weight of the picture with his shoulder to prevent it crashing to the floor, Robert draws out the screws one by one. He needn't have worried, the picture sticks to the wall, it has hung there so long, and has to be levered off. It feels surprisingly small, not that he's complaining. Quick, wrap it in the sheet, collect the tools and he's done.

Siegfried – *What are they doing to you my darling? My dearest!*
Elizabeth – *He's wrapping her in a bedsheet. He's taking her away and I can't stop him. I'm the Queen of England and I can do nothing to stop one measly little thief.*
Bess –   *Hedova! Listen to me! Don't worry. Douglas will find you. He'll bring you back.*
Siegfried – *Has he gone? Has he taken her?*
Will –   *He's taken her.*
Siegfried – *Arrrrrrrrrrrrgh!*

Robert creeps back down the stairs, taking care not to let the painting or his holdall clash against the railings. He is about to enter the foyer when he sees a figure carrying a stack of boxes walk towards the shop. He flattens himself against the wall. The caretaker has her back to him. He waits, a frozen statue, until she reaches the shop, then as she bends forward to lower the boxes onto the floor, he moves silently across the foyer and re-enters the corridor. This time he turns left, hoping to find the staff exit. Yes, as he thought, it's situated at the far end of the passage. As he gets closer he can make out a key pad. The bastards! They're not going to make it easy for him. He wasn't prepared for this. An entrance code he can understand but why block people from leaving? Robert punches in a series of numbers. No joy. He tries again, this time using the date the gallery opened. A red light flashes. He daren't try again in case he sets off a warning and the caretaker comes running to see what's going on. Now what?

Jamie is due to pick him up in five minutes. Best put him off rather than have him hanging around asking questions. Bugger! No signal. Come on, think, think. He could wait until a member of staff arrives and push past them before they have time to close the door then make a run for it. Or he could hide until the main doors open at ten, then make his escape through the front of the building. He's not keen on either of these options. There's no way of disguising the picture and he has no intention of leaving without it.

One more possibility occurs to him. What about forcing the caretaker to open the back door? He planned it earlier, how to soften her up with the chisel or screwdriver, but now it's a real possibility his stomach summersaults and he knows he couldn't do it. He sinks under the weight of bitter disappointment. It's gone so well up till now. Is it going to end in failure?

Robert hears the crunch of feet on gravel and steps back into a recess, heart racing. The door opens and someone wedges it in place with a hardback folder. Robert guesses he or she will go back to the car to collect something heavy or awkward, a piece of equipment perhaps. He'll have to be quick. He peers through the gap. Not far away a woman hums to herself as she rummages in the boot of her car. What a fantastic piece of luck! Robert opens the door wide enough to let himself, the holdall and the picture through. Dragging them behind him, he crawls towards the railings which run along one side of the car park, keeping himself hidden behind a conveniently placed row of waste bins.

Still crouching, he tries to post the painting through the iron railings but it won't go. He checked the width and height but forgot to take account of the depth of the heavily carved frame. Quick, quick! Other cars are beginning to arrive. He runs the risk of being noticed if he hangs around much longer. It has to be the hedge. Robert crawls to the point where the railings end and the hedge begins. To his relief it's formed of fairly young bushes. The growth is dense but the individual twigs provide no resistance, allowing him to push the picture through followed by the holdall. Finally he forces the branches apart and squeezes through himself. He emerges on the other side scratched and dishevelled but unharmed. A couple of minutes later Jamie arrives.

'Hop in.' Jamie gets out of the car. 'I'll put that in the boot.'

'You're okay. I'll keep it with me.' Robert slides onto the back seat keeping a tight grip on his package. 'Seven years bad luck and all that.'

'Where to?' Jamie resumes his seat and fires the engine.

'Left at the end of the road, then right at the traffic lights.' Robert realises his voice is shaking and tries to cover it up with a cough.

When they reach the traffic lights Jamie turns to look at him. 'You all right, mate?'

'Feeling a bit rough. I was very close to Uncle Ray. He was the only one left on my mum's side.'

That does the trick. Jamie puts on a sympathetic expression and says nothing more until they reach South Road.

'You can drop me off here. On the left is good.' Robert undoes his seatbelt and hotches forward in his seat as the car slows to a halt. 'What do I owe you for the petrol?' He pulls his wallet from his pocket, dislodging a shower of receipts as he does so. Shit! He retrieves what he can but some disappear into the general clutter on the floor of the car.

Jamie catches his eye in the mirror. 'Listen. I'm okay for time. I may as well take you right to the doorstep. You not feeling well and all.'

For fuck's sake! Robert doesn't need a nursemaid. All he needs is a lift.

'No thanks. Here is just fine.'

Robert watches until Jamie's car is out of sight then he slings the bag over his shoulder, picks up the picture and makes his way slowly down a little path leading to the rear of the cemetery. Halfway along he stops to punch the air.

Yes! He's done it! He's pushed himself to the edge and he hasn't cracked. He props the picture up against a tree trunk, unzips his flies and has the longest and the most satisfying piss of his life.

* * *

Douglas has to pick up some sample leaflets from the printers on his way to work. They weren't expecting him quite this early and keep him waiting while they assemble his order. He returns to find his car blocked in by one of that rapidly increasing number of drivers who think they are entitled to park wherever they choose so long so they leave the hazard lights flashing! Even then Douglas arrives at the gallery before nine. He takes the stairs to level two with the intention of putting up a sign marking the spot where his tour will start, but is waylaid by the director who emerges from the Portrait Room as Douglas comes into view.

'Ah! There you are Douglas. We've been waiting for you. Would you step in here for a moment?' His voice drops to a breathy whisper as Douglas follows him inside. 'Bad news I'm afraid. There's been a burglary! They've taken Furini's *Head of a Girl.*'

The caretaker is standing in the centre of the room, evidently in a state of shock. She points to the place where Hedova usually hangs. Douglas stares at the empty space in dismay and disbelief. 'Poor darling. She must be terrified.'

The director clears his throat more loudly than is necessary. 'Pull yourself together! We're talking about theft, not kidnapping.'

'Sorry. Silly of me, but you get surprisingly fond of these people when you see them as often as I do.'

'I know what you mean,' the caretaker is close to tears. 'I don't feel the day has started until I've said good morning to King George. Not today though. I came to check the room and found this empty space. I still can't believe it. Why would anyone want to do such a thing? It's never happened before.'

'And it won't happen again, not on my watch. This is to be kept absolutely secret. Do you both understand? The fewer people who know the better and I certainly don't want the press finding out.'

The director instructs the caretaker to take the rest of the day off. He makes it sound as if he's concerned for her well-being but Douglas guesses the real reason is he doesn't trust her to keep the news to herself while she's still in shock. Douglas offers to accompany her downstairs but she insists she'll be fine and totters off rather unsteadily towards the lift.

Left alone with Douglas, the director expands on his strategy for containing the situation.

'My primary objective has to be to see *Head of a Girl* returned to its rightful place. I've taken the decision to adhere to the gallery's default policy which is to negotiate a ransom directly with the thief without involving the police. I'll be handling that side of things.'

It strikes Douglas that the director is actually quite enjoying himself; he's behaving rather like Churchill addressing his War Cabinet.

'At the same time we'll conduct an investigation to establish the facts surrounding the theft with a view to tightening up security procedures. Douglas, I'd like you to take the lead with that. As a former deputy headmaster you must have encountered similar situations.'

'Not really, not like this.'

'Nevertheless, it's well within your capability. Officially we're not interested in finding out who stole the painting. Personally, I consider this to be a very short-sighted approach. If we don't identify the thief, we simply make ourselves an easy target in the future. So, if in the course of the investigation you come across any clues as to his identity, you have my permission to pursue them. It would be irresponsible of us not to. How does that sound?'

Douglas replies that it sounds very good but it would sound even better if he had an assistant.

'I'm not sure we can spare anyone. We're fully stretched over half-term. Unless we take someone from archives. Their work can be put on hold for the duration, none of it is urgent. Have a word with Lucy. Meanwhile we need to account for this empty space.'

Douglas suggests they tell visitors that *Head of a Girl* is on loan to another gallery for research purposes, i.e. to try to establish who painted it, and offers to put up a notice to that effect.

'Excellent suggestion. Thank you. It's all we can do for now. I should return to my office. People will wonder what's going on if I stay up here any longer. Good luck with your investigation. Don't forget to keep me up to date.' The director marches off towards the lift. Douglas can barely stop himself from clicking his heels together in a salute and shouldering his make-believe rifle.

Douglas is busy welcoming those who've signed up for his tour when he hears Bindu's wail of disappointment. He excuses himself and hurries through to the Portrait Room where Tia is pointing to the notice and explaining to her distraught granddaughter that Hedova will be back when the research is complete. She gives Douglas a reproachful look. 'You should have warned us.'

'There wasn't time. I only discovered myself this morning. It was quite a shock.'

Douglas crouches down to Bindu's level. 'You'll see her again soon and she'll be just as beautiful. Now come with me, the tour begins in five minutes. You can give me feedback. That means you can tell me what you think of it, tell me if anything needs to be improved.'

To Tia's amazement and envy Bindu stops snivelling and walks off quite calmly at Douglas's side.

Douglas begins the tour by giving a potted history of the building which dates back to the beginning of the twentieth century when it was built as a private residence for Sir Peter Whitler, an astute businessman and wealthy landowner who made his fortune from coal. Originally the house was surrounded by acres of landscaped garden but now it's hemmed in on all sides by terraced houses. Sir Peter died childless and left his home to the civic authorities who over the years have used it for a number of different purposes, including a holding place for prisoners of war, a private school and a children's hospital. In the 1970s the council began an ambitious programme of repairs and restoration and in 1980 the building was reopened as the Whitler Gallery, with a Local History Centre in the basement.

One member of the group asks a number of complicated – and in Tia's opinion irrelevant – questions and Douglas is much too polite to tell him to shut up. As they move into the Landscape Room, Bindu announces in a loud whisper that she's bored.

Tia puts her finger to her lips and whispers, '*Chhoop koro*! Be quiet!'

'I did ask her for feedback!' Douglas laughs. 'It gets better, Bindu. I promise.'

He lives up to his word. He examines a handful of paintings in great detail then explains how they relate to paintings with a similar theme from other periods. At each stage he adapts his material for the younger members of the party without being patronising. They meditate on John Constable's *Study of Clouds* and experience the excitement of *Boar Hunt* from the studio of Peter Paul Rubens. Douglas welcomes comments, both the obvious and the obscure, from the audience. After the last visitors have left Douglas asks Bindu for her verdict. She tells him it was mostly good but she couldn't concentrate because she was talking to Hedova, asking her to come back quickly.

Tia dismisses the idea as nonsense. 'You can't talk to a picture!'

Douglas says, 'I beg to disagree. I often have a chat with Will and Bess. They don't answer but they do listen.'

This sounds to Tia suspiciously like religion, putting your faith in someone or something you created in the first place then kidding yourself it cares about you. She's surprised someone as intelligent as Douglas subscribes to it. Well, if it comforts him to talk to some squares of canvas covered in paint, then let him get on with it, only she'd rather he didn't encourage Bindu to do the same. Tia went through a religious spell herself, when things were really bad with her husband. Devotee of Sai Baba, Theravada Buddhist, Jehovah's Witness, Pagan, she tried the lot and came to the firm conclusion they are all based on self-deception and wishful thinking.

Now that his tour is complete Douglas can relax. 'Let me buy you each an ice cream.'

Tia won't hear of it. It's almost time for lunch.

He smiles persuasively. 'Couldn't you do it the other way round – just this once?'

'Just this once tends to become a habit,' Tia says brusquely.

That's how it started, her husband's so-called illness. One more glass, one more bottle, just this once; because his team won the match, because they were on holiday, because it was someone's birthday, because someone had died, because he couldn't stop, because he couldn't function without it. She told people he had liver disease; she didn't say it was alcoholic hepatitis.

She says, 'I'll buy us all lunch, then you can buy the ice creams for dessert.'

Douglas consults Bindu. 'What do you think? Would you like me to join you for lunch?'

Tia wonders why he's asking Bindu, as if she has some control over who Tia has lunch with. Fortunately, Bindu doesn't raise any objection. Douglas proves to be a brilliant lunch guest. He puts as much effort into entertaining Tia and Bindu as he puts into conducting his tour. Bindu eats very little of her cheeseburger – her excuse is she's missing Hedova – but makes short work of a giant ice cream.

'So you call your grandmother Thakuma. What do you call your grandfather?'

'I haven't got a grandfather.'

Douglas looks enquiringly at Tia.

'My husband died nine years ago, before Bindu was born.' There is an awkward silence. Tia does not wish to expand. She gets to her feet and passes Bindu her jacket.

'Thank you, Douglas. We've had a lovely time. Haven't we Bindu?'

Bindu doesn't reply.

'Bindu, is there something you want to say?'

Bindu frowns. 'What?'

'I was saying, we've had a lovely time, haven't we?'

'I suppose.'

Before they part Douglas asks Tia for her mobile number.

* * *

Robert finds the cemetery gate and follows the pitted tarmac path until he reaches a boarded-up chapel and an imposing monument, rising well above the surrounding graves and featuring a pair of Greek urns, in remembrance of Sir Peter Whitler. That's neat. He's about to hide a picture he's stolen from the Whitler Gallery in the cemetery where the original owner of the gallery building is buried!

Robert branches off to the left across the grass. The burials are scattered randomly with no pathways between. He treads cautiously but every so often the ground collapses and his feet sink into someone's skeleton, or that's what he imagines anyway. Huge trees, nourished by the flesh and bones of the deceased, spread their branches wide so no rays of sunshine reach the graves. Tree roots have cracked the walls of sepulchres and dislodged crosses and headstones.

Everything that is meant to be upright leans to one side or has fallen flat on its face.

Robert reaches a large black headstone, raised on a pedestal and with an angel carved out of marble sitting on the top. Resting the picture on the ground he reads the inscription. He reads it a couple more times to make sure he's got it right. Andrew, poor sod, had to watch his first son die then his wife and finally his second son.

> Here lies the body of Andrew Oliver
> who d 2nd July 1895 aged 48 y
> And his dear wife Mary
> who d 12th Nov 1880 aged 30 y
> And their sons Peter
> who d 5th April 1870 aged 2 y
> And James
> who d 3rd Dec 1886 aged 16 y
> *The Lord giveth and the Lord taketh away*

Robert looks around for a place to hide the picture. Some of the graves have little raised walls along the boundary. Where a tombstone has fallen forward onto one of these, the result is similar to a lid on a box. It might be possible to slide the picture into the empty space and pull the tombstone over it. He spots one grave that looks suitable and goes over to try. The picture slides in easily enough but manoeuvring the tombstone into position is more difficult. It's heavier than he expected and doesn't want to budge. The friction between two rough surfaces is too great and he's on the point of giving up when he discovers that by swinging the tombstone first one way then the other, he can move it forward inch by inch until the picture is entirely hidden.

Robert dumps the balaclava and gloves in a waste bin just inside the cemetery gate. He's halfway down the path leading to the main road when he stops and turns back. Best get rid of the holdall too; he was carrying it when he arrived at the gallery on Tuesday afternoon and the CCTV cameras might have picked it up. He slides the screwdriver and chisel up his sleeve and holds them in place with a clenched fist then sets off to walk the half-hour journey back to his flat. Then he remembers. What a wally! He left the baseball cap and his dad's scarf in the stockroom. And the towels – he meant to collect the towels before coming down the stairs. Do fingerprints show up on cloth, or only on hard surfaces? He's not sure. They'll get a surprise if they discover his deceased father's prints! Nothing he can do about it now.

It's midday when Robert arrives at his flat. His face and arms are covered in scratches, his hands are grazed and bruised and his nails are torn. He's totally knackered and dizzy with hunger but well satisfied. He eats three packets of crisps and falls asleep on the sofa.

Siegfried – *My heart aches. I can't bear it. Will I ever see my darling again?*

Amy – *Love brings more suffering than joy. I learned that lesson very young. In fact I died learning it.*

Bess – *You're not helping, Amy. That kind of talk only makes it worse. We can't give up hope. We have to stay positive.*

Will – *Douglas will track down the thief if anyone can.*

Bess –   Ordinarily I would agree with you. But right now his mind is on other things!

Will –   How do you mean?

Bess –   He fancies Bindu's grandmother. Can't you tell?

Will –   That's going too far! Douglas likes her, yes, but that's all. He genuinely thinks she'll make a good assistant.

Bess –   I think it goes a bit deeper than that.

Will –   I have no doubt Douglas will carry out a thorough investigation.

Bess –   But will he be successful? It's not enough to be thorough. We need a result.

Elizabeth – If they do catch the thief he'll plead temporary insanity. His brief will get him off with a few weeks' community service. In my time men lost their heads for lesser crimes, picking pockets and poaching for example.

Bess –   It would never have happened to me. I kept a night watchman to guard my property, not to mention the dogs.

Will –   In my day they'd deport him to the American colonies.

Bess –   The man entered a public building and stole a valuable object. If you ask me, for that he deserves to be hung, drawn and quartered in public.

Amy –   He won't come back will he, the thief? He won't come back and pick us off one by one?

Will –   Now see what you've done. The poor woman's terrified.

Elizabeth – Don't let her fool you. She's pleased to see the back of Hedova. I've seen the way she looks at Siegfried.

Amy –   How can you say such a thing!
Elizabeth – I'm the Queen of England. I'll say what I like.
Tia doesn't hear the doorbell when Subir arrives to collect
Bindu that evening. He has to knock on the window to
attract her attention. Most unusual. Any other day Tia
would have Bindu ready and waiting on the doorstep.
But today her emotions are jumbled up, her hormones
(what's left of them) are working overtime, and she can't do
anything about it. She doesn't want to do anything about it.

Why did Douglas ask for her phone number? Does
there have to be a reason? Tia and her friends often phone
each other for no other reason than to chat. But with men
there usually is a reason. Does Douglas have romantic
intentions? It's an intriguing idea. So far as Tia knows no
one has entertained romantic intentions towards her for at
least ten years. She wonders sometimes why that is, and why
she hasn't felt attracted to anyone. Throughout her marriage
she had a tendency to flirt, nothing serious just a bit of fun.

Like the rather sweet pharmacist who always made sure he
served her personally when she went to collect her husband's
medication. She didn't step aside when he reached across her
to the shelf where dispensed prescriptions were stored, and he
let his fingers linger a little longer than was necessary when he
passed the bag to her. Or the handyman she appointed to do
odd jobs around the house and garden because her husband
wouldn't. While she was explaining what needed to be done,
he ran his eyes over her body and instead of shrinking from
his gaze she ran her eyes over his. But that's a long time back.
Tia can't remember when she last fancied anyone.

Not that she's looking for a relationship. She doesn't
want a man clogging up her life! Complaining about the

meals she cooks and the clothes she wears and the friends she goes out with and the way she spends her money. She's escaped from all that and isn't going to give up her independence, however charming the suitor.

* * *

It's hunger that finally wakes Robert up. He hasn't eaten since Tuesday lunchtime, thirty hours ago, and his stomach is screaming for food. He goes to stand up but his legs give way and he drops back onto the sofa. During the night he spent squashed between two cupboards in the stockroom, he twisted and pulled every muscle in his body and the struggle to move the headstone into place made it worse. Holding onto the back of the sofa then walking his hands along the wall Robert makes it to the kitchen, by which time the stiffness in his spine and limbs has eased a little and he can stand upright. He drinks a glass of water and then another. On Tuesday he deliberately cut down on fluids knowing he wouldn't be able to piss during the night.

It's six in the evening. He has just carried out a successful robbery, the first step in his new career as an art thief. He planned and did the job himself and wasn't fazed when obstacles arose. The picture is safely stashed away until it's given back to the gallery in return for a decent sum of money. So why is he sitting alone in his flat? Why isn't he out there celebrating?

He needs someone to celebrate with, right? He can't do it on his own. But because of the nature of the thing he's celebrating he has to keep it to himself. That doesn't stop him going out for a drink and a meal with a mate; Robert will know what he's celebrating even if his companion doesn't. He can't for the life of him think of anyone he can phone, let alone at the last minute. There's an ex-girlfriend from way back, the only girlfriend Robert has ever had and she only lasted one week. She might say yes but he doesn't want her getting the wrong idea. Anyway he's heard rumours that she's married.

A couple of lads from work might be up for it but Robert doesn't want to spend the evening listening to them banging on about what they'd like to do to the female supervisors and complaining about the low rates paid for working overtime. He decides to go out in any case and if he bumps into someone he knows, well that will be a bonus. He might even make friends with someone new.

It takes Robert a long time to get washed and changed. Although he irons his clothes before he hangs them in the wardrobe, they always seem to be in need of reironing when he comes to put them on. He irons everything he wears; jeans, T-shirt, vest, boxers, socks. He's even been known to iron his shoelaces if they won't lie flat. When he's ready he stands in front of the mirror. He can feel his dad's hand on his shoulder, congratulating him. Robert descends the staircase two steps at a time.

Six o'clock on Wednesday evening is not a popular slot in the week for socialising. Most people are hurrying back home to their families, stopping to pick up supplies as they pass the supermarket on the way to the car park or station. Robert smiles at everyone he passes; one or two people smile back but mostly they're too preoccupied with their own stuff. Robert is determined not to let this dampen his spirits and starts greeting everyone with 'good evening' or 'how you doing?' or simply 'hi' according to how old they are and whether they are male or female. One chap gets shirty when Robert directs a cheery, 'hello' in his direction.

'Who you talking to?'

Robert answers with a wide smile.

'I'm warning you, keep away from my girlfriend!'

Jealous git. Why should Robert be interested in his girlfriend? Ah! One look at the leggy blonde hanging onto the man's arm and Robert can see why. Her boyfriend is still glaring at him. A couple of lads stop to see how the matter will develop. Other curious bystanders join them. Encouraged by the audience the man with the girlfriend threatens to teach Robert a lesson. Robert holds up his hand in surrender and quickly crosses the road.

Robert makes his way to a street where every other building is a restaurant. It's an area he has often wanted to explore but up till now he hasn't had the courage. Robert is not adventurous where eating is concerned and still thinks twice before consuming chow mein or vindaloo, but today is a day of firsts. It's good to feel he's surrounded by food from around the world – Italian, Thai, Lebanese, Taiwanese, Greek, Japanese, South Indian, Mexican. He reads the menus displayed in the windows, trying to guess what the different dishes taste like, and finally plumps for a restaurant that serves a number of English dishes alongside the less familiar ones.

Of course what Robert thinks of as traditional was once itself new. Elizabeth I, Bess of Hardwick and Amy Robsart were amongst the first to eat potatoes, now a staple component of the English diet. Sir William Craven ate herbs and strong cheeses and crusty bread brought here by the Huguenots, and George III welcomed tomatoes and citrus fruits as newcomers to the royal table.

The waiter greets Robert at the restaurant door.

'Table for one, or are you waiting for someone to join you?'

'Nope! There's only me.' That makes him sound like a sad git. 'My wife was planning to come with me but she's been called away unexpectedly. Father's unwell.'

'I'm sorry to hear that.'

Robert doesn't want anyone feeling sorry for him. 'She said I was to celebrate just the same.'

'Celebrate?'

'It's my birthday.'

The waiter leads him to a table beside the window. Robert orders half a lager and glances round the room. All the other tables are empty except for one ancient couple in the corner, American judging by their jazzy clothes and raucous voices. Robert spreads a paper serviette over his knees and picks up the menu. He is tempted by the steak and kidney pie but is determined to choose something different this time, seeing as it's a special occasion. The gammon looks good but it's so salty. A steak? Better not, all that red meat is bad for his heart, besides it bungs up his insides. Fish perhaps. He likes salmon but not when it's swimming in a slimy sauce. Chicken is too common; he can eat chicken any time he likes.

* * *

Douglas sends a text before phoning, asking Tia if now is a good time. Typical of him to be so considerate. Tia texts back saying could he wait ten minutes while she finishes her dinner? He gives her precisely eleven minutes then makes the call.

'I hope you enjoyed your meal?'

'I did, thank you.'

'It's very rude of me to ask but I'd love to know what you had.'

'Yes. Very rude.'

'I do apologise. I was only—'

'I'm teasing! I had salmon cooked with mustard seeds and chilli, *toor* dal and rice.'

'You're making my mouth water!'

'You must come over one day. I'll cook for you.' It is just one of those things people say. Nothing will come of it.

'I expect you're wondering why I phoned. I could have spoken to you this afternoon but I thought it best to wait till you could give me your full attention. Before I go any further I need you to understand that everything I say is highly confidential. Is that all right?'

'If you mean can I keep a secret, the answer is yes, I can.'

'Hedova hasn't been sent away for examination, that's only a story we concocted. She wasn't hanging in the Portrait Room when the caretaker arrived this morning. No sign of her anywhere. She's been stolen!'

Tia can't make sense of it at first. Then it dawns on her, his phone call relates to the gallery, to be precise to the theft of a painting, and has nothing whatsoever to do with romantic intentions. It takes Tia a few moments to get over her surprise and disappointment and see the funny side. But when she does, she has to bury her face in a cushion to stifle her laughter. Thank goodness they're on the phone, not face to face!

'Are you okay?'

'I'm fine, but you must be upset. You were very fond of that picture, weren't you?'

'I'd rather you didn't use the past tense. I'm still very fond of Hedova's portrait. We'll get it back sooner or later. The director is waiting for the thief to get in touch so he can negotiate a ransom.'

'You mean the gallery will just pay up and that's it? We won't tell the police?'

'The governors aren't interested in catching the thief, only in getting the picture back. So far as they're concerned, he can walk away with the ransom.'

'And never be punished for what he's done?'

'That's correct.'

'That can't be right.'

'The director would agree with you. He wants to find out who stole Hedova and he's asked me to lead the investigation, only we can't call it that; officially it's a review of security procedures. Naturally I accepted but I need an assistant. He suggested I choose someone from archives and I'm choosing you. Will you do it?'

For a few moments Tia doesn't know what to say. She's flattered, of course, and would like to be of help, particularly when the person asking is Douglas.

'I've never done anything like it before. I'm not sure how much help I'd be.'

'You're intelligent, you can think for yourself and won't be afraid to tell me if I get it wrong. That sounds to me like a pretty good list of qualifications. Do please say yes. It's not every day you get the chance to play detective!'

As before, when they were in the Portrait Room, Tia finds Douglas's enthusiasm contagious. 'I'll do it but you'll have to talk to Lucy.'

'I've already spoken to her. I've been waiting for her to get back to me and now she has. She's prepared to release you for up to a fortnight if we need it.'

Bubbles of excited anticipation explode in Tia's chest. 'Okay, so when do we start?'

'Immediately. How are you fixed for tomorrow?'

'Bindu is with me all day. I'll ask my friend if she can look after her.'

'Time is of the essence. We can't let the trail grow cold. Come in at nine if you can and we'll put our heads together.' Pause. 'So to speak. I've already sent round an email asking staff to let us know if they've seen anything unusual or suspicious recently. And I've let the security firm know we want to view the CCTV footage.'

Tia is excited at the prospect. She doesn't often get excited, not anymore. Crucial question: what's she going to wear? For a while now she's lived in jeans and trainers; investigating a theft calls for a more professional look. She'll be working with Douglas and he's always impeccably turned out. What starts as a quick rifle through the wardrobe to pick out something to wear tomorrow rapidly turns into a major clear-out. Anything that no longer fits or hasn't been worn for a couple of years is ironed and put aside for the Children's Hospice shop. Having tried a number of different combinations Tia selects the peacock-blue silk fitted top with tapered black trousers. Smart but not severe. Just right for the part. She can't wait to get started.

* * *

While he's waiting for someone to come and take his order, Robert studies the pictures hanging on the restaurant walls. Most of them are prints, but the one beside the till looks like an original. It's a painting of the city centre as it was a hundred years ago. He'd love to have it hanging on his bedroom wall. He may decide not to ransom all the pictures he steals, he might keep a few. That will give him the chance to study them carefully and see how it's done. Perhaps he'll branch out into art fraud. Make copies which look exactly like the original so no one can tell the difference. That way he'll get double the profit. So long as he has a steady hand and pays attention to every tiny detail surely it should be possible to copy any picture.

The waiter brings Robert's drink and takes his order – steak and kidney pie with an assortment of green vegetables. The American couple are between courses and come over for a chat. Robert discovers they are actually Geordies. He never was any good with accents.

'We're supposed to be visiting our daughter but we've spent most of our time looking at trains, haven't we, pet?' says the long-suffering wife.

It turns out the man is a real fanatic; he did the *Eastern Oriental Express*, Singapore to Bangkok, last year which has Robert grinding his teeth with envy. Robert considers claiming he's done the Trans-Siberian but they'd probably guess he was lying so he sings the praises of the Carlisle to Settle line instead. True, Robert's never actually done the Carlisle to Settle trip but he's seen enough documentaries on it to sound as if he's an authority.

The man notices Robert's hands. 'What happened?'

'I had an argument with a rose bush!'

'You should put antiseptic cream on them or they'll get infected,' says the wife who turns out to be a retired district nurse.

Robert is disappointed when the waiter delivers his meal. It's not really a pie, just a square of pastry dumped on top of a beef stew (the two tiny pieces of kidney hardly count). Serves him right, he should have been more adventurous. Things will be different when he's up and running, with his own contacts and outlets. He'll eat snails and squid and snake then, without batting an eyelid. And he'll ride a Harley Davidson, a long-standing dream, and own a cottage in the country. The ransom Robert gets for Samuel Baker should be enough for a deposit on a cottage. He'll go to the estate agents tomorrow and see what's available.

The restaurant is beginning to fill up. As Robert finishes his main course the Geordie couple sip the last of their coffee and struggle into their coats. The waiter brings them their bill which they pay by card but instead of leaving they make their way to Robert's table. To his acute embarrassment the waiter emerges from the kitchen carrying a miniature strawberry cheesecake with a single candle burning amongst the glazed fruits. The Geordies sing 'Happy Birthday' in tremulous voices and the other diners join in, craning their necks to see who they're singing to. Despite his embarrassment Robert is touched; he can't remember the last time anyone sang 'Happy Birthday' to him.

'We couldn't finish our wine,' the ex-nurse says as she puts the half-finished bottle on Robert's table. 'So sorry your wife couldn't be with you. I hope her father recovers quickly.'

Robert is ashamed. He wants to confess that it's not his birthday and he isn't married. Instead he thanks them for their kindness and hopes they enjoy the rest of their trip.

Later, Robert's footsteps reverberate off concrete walls as he walks back to his flat carrying the remains of the cheesecake in a doggy bag. Not exactly what he had in mind as a celebration but overall a pleasant enough way to spend the evening. Tomorrow he must phone the gallery and discuss the ransom. But for now it's an early night, the excitement of the last three days has caught up with him.

CHAPTER FOUR

When Subir comes to drop Bindu off next day, Tia tells him something urgent has come up at work.

'It's okay for Bindu to come with me to the gallery for the morning then I'll take her round to Shompa's for the afternoon.'

'Three days of playing Thakuma and you've had enough, is that it? Can't someone else cover for you? I thought you wanted to play a more significant role in your granddaughter's life.'

Subir's reproof hurts. He makes it sound as if it's a choice between work and family, between honouring her commitment to the gallery and being a good Thakuma to Bindu. That's unfair. Tia has a genuine reason for making the arrangement and Bindu won't come to any harm while she's with Shompa. Although he pretends to be annoyed Tia knows Subir is actually relieved to hear his daughter will spend time with a 'normal' family. He's already complained that Bindu's obsession with Hedova is driving Putul mad.

Tia says, 'Listen, *shona*. You're going to Shompa auntie's house later. That's good isn't it? You can play with her grandsons.'

No tearful protest. No angry refusal. Tia should be pleased that Bindu is gaining confidence, and in a way she is, but she's also disappointed. Part of her would love Bindu to say, 'I'm not going to Shompa auntie's. I want to stay with you, Thakuma.'

Douglas stands in the foyer waiting eagerly for Tia and Bindu to arrive. What a lovely woman! It's a shame he hasn't had much to do with her up till now. She's blessed with good looks – Sophia Loren without the glamour – as well as a cheerful disposition and a sharp sense of humour. She possesses the easy confidence of one untroubled by self-doubt and Douglas is delighted at the prospect of being daily in her company for at least a week, maybe longer; it depends on how their enquiries progress. He's kept himself busy the last two years and has much to be thankful for, not least for Will and Bess, but if he's honest it's been a lonely journey. Having someone like Tia, energetic but not too intense, to work alongside is exactly the tonic he needs.

Douglas catches sight of them as they approach the main entrance. Tia moves with the grace and suppleness of a natural athlete while Bindu is tucked close in her wake. Douglas waves with both arms to attract their attention. Tia's face breaks into a smile as she spots him.

'Good to see you! I hope you're both well?'

'I'm not,' Bindu says.

'Sorry to hear that.' Douglas looks at Tia for clarification.

'First I've heard of it.'

'But I told you, Thakuma. I told you I didn't sleep all night. Why don't you listen?'

Tia wonders if Bindu is deliberately undermining her in front of Douglas.

Douglas says he is very sorry Bindu is not feeling well, but he's sure she'll feel better if she gets involved in one of the morning activities for children. He runs through the list and asks which one she'd like to sign up for. Tia suspects he's wasting his time and she's right; even with Douglas and Tia both doing their best to persuade her, Bindu won't try any of the workshops.

How different from her father! When Subir was young he joined everything on offer. Choir, debating club, dramatic society, chess association. His sister was the same. They met life head on whereas Bindu turns inwards or runs away. Their success didn't just happen, they had to put in the effort. Tia worries that her granddaughter is fast becoming one of those people who expects to be handed success on a plate and goes into a huff when it isn't.

'No problem, you can stay with us,' Douglas says. 'I'm sure I can find something for you to do.'

Evie is watching with amusement from the information desk. 'You here again? I thought you were supposed to be on leave.'

Tia shrugs. 'I know. Sad isn't it? I love my job so much I just can't keep away!'

They follow Douglas to the Volunteers' Room situated on the first floor of the admin block. This is to be their headquarters for the duration of the investigation. The room is distinctly shabby. It contains a kettle, a sink, a table-top fridge, an odd assortment of rather dodgy chairs and a coffee table with a wonky leg. The carpet is badly stained and there are marks on the walls where someone has stuck sticky tape.

'There's something I'd really like you to do for me, Bindu.' Douglas places a large jar of assorted paper clips on the table. 'These need sorting into sizes. Can you do that please?'

Bindu obediently throws herself onto the floor and begins separating the clips into piles.

'Coffee?' Douglas turns somewhat doubtfully to Tia who pulls a face. 'I thought not. Doesn't look very enticing does it?'

He delves into his briefcase and pulls out a notebook. At the top of the first page he writes 'An investigation into the theft of *Head of a Girl* (aka Hedova) from the Portrait Room in the Whitler Gallery' and underlines it. Then he pushes the notebook and pen towards Tia.

'Would you keep a daily record of our progress? I tend to get carried away and forget to write things down.'

Tia wonders if he's giving her a job to keep her happy, rather like asking Bindu to sort the paper clips! She takes the pen and writes "Evidence". Together they review what they know so far. They know the picture was there at 17:30 on Tuesday because the caretaker saw it when she did her final round before locking up. They also know the picture was missing at 08:45 on Wednesday when the caretaker went into the Portrait Room to adjust the temperature.

'We know the external alarm didn't go off, nor the alarms which monitor the internal doors. The caretaker is fairly sure no one has meddled with any part of the security system. Oh, and we know there is no sign of anybody breaking in or breaking out.' Tia looks at Douglas doubtfully. 'Does that count as evidence? Things that didn't happen rather than things that did.'

'It certainly does. Evidence can be commission and omission. Presence and absence. Not everybody has the wits to appreciate that.' Douglas goes over to the window. 'I can't understand how the thief got into the gallery and then out again carrying the picture. We must have missed something.'

'That sounds to me like speculation. Let's stick with the evidence for now.' Tia scribbles in the notebook. 'We know the thief used towels to cover the CCTV cameras and that he – for now let's assume it's a man – left the towels behind.'

'We don't have CCTV footage of the actual theft but there may be something of interest on the tapes when we study them.' Douglas resumes his seat. 'That's about it for evidence.'

Bindu says, 'What about that man I saw taking photos?'

Tia didn't believe Bindu at the time but in the light of subsequent events she may have to revise her judgement. 'What did he look like? Can you describe him?'

'He looked like Mr Goodall, that's a teacher in my school. Not very tall. A bit fat so you wouldn't think he can run fast but he can. And a friendly sort of face.'

Douglas congratulates her on her powers of observation. He runs through some general principles for carrying out investigations. Most of them are fairly obvious: accept nothing at face value, keep an open mind, the source of the evidence is as important as the evidence itself, don't ask too many questions.

'I don't understand the last one,' says Tia. 'I thought detectives were supposed to ask questions.'

'That's true but it's not all about questions. You have to give the person you're interviewing the chance to tell you things they consider important, things you hadn't even thought of. I can remember investigating an instance of arson without being aware the father of the pupil who found the fire and reported it, had recently been convicted of sexual assault and GBH.'

'Why would that make a difference?'

'It made the boy extremely volatile. I would have suspected him straight away if I'd known that. Looking back on it I realise he tried to tell me but I wouldn't listen. I had him down as the good guy.'

'What happened?'

'He confessed and was given a caution on a plea of mitigating circumstances.'

'That's all? Surely if he did it then he should be punished. Full stop.'

Douglas launches into a spirited defence of mitigating circumstances. Tia holds up her hand.

'You're losing focus. Can we save that for later?'

Douglas looks at her hand – small, supple and decisive. He smiles. 'You're right. We mustn't lose focus.'

* * *

The night after his solitary celebration Robert wakes abruptly, dripping with sweat. It's only three o'clock but he can't get back to sleep. He's convinced "Wanted" posters showing his face are being projected onto tall buildings across the city. He saw them clearly, leering at him and threatening to tell everyone where he lived. But that's not possible; they can't have checked the CCTV cameras that quickly, let alone designed and distributed the poster. It must have been a bad dream. All the same it makes sense to disguise himself and it would be good to do it before morning. Robert fetches his electric shaver, extends the trimmer head and applies it to the top of his head. It makes little impression. He'll have to cut the hair with scissors first, as short as he can. He brings a pair from the kitchen and gets to work, pulling up a tuft with one hand and cutting it as close to the scalp as possible with the other. The back of his head is more difficult, he can't hold a mirror and a tuft of hair and a pair of sharp scissors all at the same time, so he forgets about the mirror and feels his way the best he can.

At times like this he feels the need of a companion. Not just to help him shave his head, although that would be useful, but someone who he can talk to about what is going on. Someone who is really interested. Like when he sees a particularly good movie. If he went to see it with someone else they could tell each other what they liked and didn't like about it. Or like buying himself an ice cream. It would be good to have someone with him who chose a different flavour so they could taste each other's and compare. Problem is, the better you get to know someone, the less likely they are to take an interest or listen, that's been Robert's experience anyway.

When Robert has reduced all the hair on his head to a manageable though uneven length he presses the button on his shaver. Nothing. The effing battery is dead. If he puts it on charge now it'll be ready in the morning. It takes him half an hour to sweep up all the hair. He can't imagine why people keep dogs. Robert would really like to have a shower but it's not yet four o'clock and the neighbours might complain, so he makes do with a wash and a change of T-shirt before going back to bed.

The next thing he knows, it's ten o'clock and someone is hammering his front door. Robert stumbles into the hall. Jamie stands in the doorway staring at Robert as if he's broken the law by having a lie-in.

'Yes?'

'Sorry. I've disturbed you. I came round to say one of my mates has a spare ticket for the game tonight. I wondered if you'd be interested in going.'

Robert doesn't want to be too pally, considering what Jamie already knows. He might just let something slip and regret it later. So he says thanks for asking but no thanks he doesn't feel like going to the match.

'Listen mate, if you want to talk about it, I mean about your uncle, just let me know.'

'My uncle?' Robert frowns. Then suddenly remembers. 'Oh, you mean Uncle Ray. Thanks for the offer but I'm fine. Honestly.'

Jamie walks thoughtfully back to his flat. If he didn't know better he'd say the man was mentally unstable. Why would anyone want to do that to their hair? And how come Robert forgot about his uncle's death when only yesterday he collected a mirror from his uncle's house?

It's not until he passes the hall mirror that Robert realises why Jamie looked so surprised. He picks up the newly charged shaver. What's it to be, close shave or something more exciting? He cuts a wiggly line on the left side and another on the right to match. It looks good! He adds a couple more each side and then a series of straight lines, well, straight as he can manage, across the back. The result is a bit like a field after a couple of quad bikes have driven through it. Best shave it all off, he doesn't want to draw attention to himself.

* * *

Someone knocks the door of the Volunteers' Room. Douglas goes to open it but Tia is there before him. The director's PA informs them that something unusual has been found in the stockroom and would they please come and see for themselves. The three of them follow the PA's precariously high heels to the site of the discovery. The items in question are a baseball cap and a scarf. They were discovered by one of the shop assistants ten minutes ago, lying on the stockroom floor between two steel cabinets.

'When was the last time anyone came into the stockroom?' Tia enquires.

'Yesterday lunchtime. We were running out of fridge magnets to sell in the shop so I came to see whether we had any left.'

'And are you certain the cap and the scarf weren't here then?'

The shop assistant ponders a while before answering. 'I would have noticed, I'm sure I would.'

'Who else comes in here, apart from the shop staff?'

'No one. Except the caretaker.'

Douglas asks if they each have their own key.

'The door isn't locked.'

Tia and Douglas exchange glances. This seems very lax.

'Did you notice anything else unusual? Has anything been moved? Is anything missing?'

The assistant shakes her head. 'So far as we can tell, nothing's been taken. Some of the merchandise is quite valuable. Whoever it was missed a trick there.'

Douglas asks the director's PA to arrange for the cap and scarf to be placed in separate plastic bags without handling them directly, in case there's ever a question of

WHAT'S GOING ON AT THE WHITLER?

fingerprints. And could she please arrange for the cafe to send two coffees, an assortment of cakes, and an orange juice to the Volunteers' Room?

When they return to HQ, Tia adds 'baseball cap and scarf' under the heading 'Evidence'.

Douglas leans forward, chin resting in his hands, eyes half closed. 'Now it's time to speculate, come up with questions and possible solutions. I'll start. If the cap and scarf belong to the thief – remember we have no proof they do – that means the thief was in the stockroom at some point after midday yesterday. What was he doing?'

Tia says, 'If you're right then how come the caretaker didn't find the cap and scarf when she did her evening rounds?'

'Perhaps she didn't check thoroughly that night. Or perhaps he was hiding in another part of the building and went into the stockroom at some point during the night.'

'That would have triggered the room alarms.' Tia reminds him. 'More likely he came in early morning, immediately after the caretaker released the alarm, stole the picture and made himself scarce.'

Douglas interlocks his fingers and bends them back. 'That won't work either. Unless he knew the door code. Anyway wouldn't the caretaker notice if someone else was in the building? She'd hear him, at least.'

They break off to accept delivery of the refreshments. Bindu helps herself to two pieces of cake and resumes her work with the paper clips which seems to have ceased being a sorting exercise and morphed into an elaborate sculpture.

'We keep going round and round in circles and getting nowhere. We need a fresh approach. An injection of new ideas.' Tia crosses her legs and jiggles her left foot, a habit she's developed when she needs to concentrate. 'We're assuming the thief is unknown to us. What if it's an inside job? That would explain how he got in and out. How many people know the code for the external alarm?'

Douglas looks miserable. He doesn't want to confront the possibility that a member of staff is involved. 'The director and his PA, Lucy, the cafe manager and the caretaker. But I do hope you're wrong. They're such lovely people.'

Tia laughs. 'I don't think that matters! We have to keep an open mind remember?' She studies her notes as she sips her coffee. 'We're no nearer to knowing how or when he did it but we know what we don't know. Does that make sense?'

'Perfect sense. We have identified the obstacles and opened up possible lines of enquiry. That's what I would expect at this stage. You're good at this.' Douglas looks at Tia with admiration.

She says, 'It's kind of you to say so. I put it down to reading Satyajit Ray's *Complete Adventures of Feluda.*'

Bindu sits cross-legged on the floor with her head in her hands. 'I'll never see her again.'

'See who again?'

'Hedova of course. You don't know where she is, do you?'

Douglas says, 'No we don't know where she is but we're doing our best to find her.'

Tia tries to give Bindu a hug but Bindu pushes her away.

Siegfried – What news? Does anyone know if they are any closer to finding Hedova?

Will –   They have made plans to apprehend the thief but
             it's early days.

Siegfried – I'm not interested in catching the thief I just
             want to know where my poor darling is and if
             she's safe.

Elizabeth – She'll be well looked after, you can be sure of
             that. Otherwise she'd lose her value which would
             defeat the purpose of stealing her.

Amy –   Poor Hedova! She's frightened and lonely and
             doesn't know what's going on.

Elizabeth – We've told you before. That kind of talk doesn't
             help anyone. Siegfried has to stay strong. I don't
             know what he sees in Hedova personally.

Will –   Men fall for helpless women. They like to feel
             they're needed.

Bess –   What news of Douglas's love life? Did he
             reveal anything about his relationship with the
             grandmother?

Elizabeth – Why do you insist on calling her 'the grandmother'
             when she has a perfectly good name?

Will –   Tia is helping Douglas with the investigation and
             making an excellent job of it but I didn't pick up
             any undertones of romance. I admit I never was
             sensitive to such things. Buildings were my forte.
             Rebuilding the West Wing at Coombe Abbey
             consumed all my energy.

Bess –   There's an American soap called The West Wing.
             Never watched it myself but I gather it's very
             good.

Amy –   Did Douglas say anything about the little girl, I
             mean Bindu?

Will –   Only that she carries her photo of Hedova
            everywhere she goes, and keeps it under her
            pillow when she sleeps.

Amy –   Bless!

Bess –   Poor child! Tia is more interested in chasing our
            Douglas than looking after her granddaughter.

Elizabeth – I seem to remember you did your fair share of
            chasing.

Will –   Enough of that! Let's hope we get Hedova back
            soon, then we can all be happy.

* * *

After he's cleaned up the hair for the second time and been
in the shower, Robert makes himself some porridge and sits
down to plan his next move. How long should he leave it
before contacting the gallery? Is it safe to use his mobile
or will they be able to trace him? He could use his mum's
phone. He never got round to cancelling the contract and
he knows how to make the number show up as unknown.
He doesn't trust email, spies everywhere. The alternative is
to do it all by letter, but that will take a very long time.

The prospect of making the call scares Robert almost
as much as the thought of stealing the picture. He has a
habit of muddling his words and making a fool of himself.
He practises the conversation in his head but keeps drying
up or forgetting what he wants to say. Perhaps he should
write himself a script. He makes a few attempts but none
is satisfactory. He is distracted by the sight of his injured
hands and hopes Jamie didn't notice them. Robert takes a
fresh sheet of paper and tries again.

It's afternoon before he's ready to make the call. He punches in the gallery number and waits. Shite! He should disguise his voice, why didn't he think of it earlier? He could have practised. Bass is good. Deep voices give the impression the speaker has authority and deserves respect; he'll make his voice as low as he can manage.

'Thank you for calling the Whitler Gallery. My name is Evie. How can I help you today?'

The voice sounds familiar. He's pretty sure it belongs to the woman who sold him the raffle tickets. He growls, 'I'd like to speak to your boss.'

'Do you have a name?'

Of course he's got a name! What's she playing at? 'I don't want to give you my name, I want to speak to your boss.'

'I mean do you know the name of the person you wish to speak to? It would help if I had a name.'

'Just put me through to the boss. You know, the person in charge of the gallery. And don't keep me waiting.' In his frustration he forgets bass, but only for a moment. Hopefully she didn't notice.

'Very well, sir. I'll see if the director is available.' Classical music. Silence. More classical music. 'I'm sorry sir but the director is on another call. Would you like to leave a message?'

'Just say Samuel wants to talk to him. He'll understand. I'll phone back in ten minutes and he'd better be free then or you'll be sorry.' Robert ends the call. That's telling them! He counts off the minutes then calls again. Evie answers.

'Thank you for calling…'

Remember, deep voice. 'Put me through to the director.'

'Can I ask who's speaking?'

'You can ask but I won't tell you. Just put me through.'

'The director is in a meeting right now. I'm sorry.'

'Did you give him my message?'

'Which message was that, sir?'

'About Samuel.'

'Yes, sir, I gave him that message but he doesn't know anyone called Samuel.'

They're playing silly buggers with him. They must know he's talking about Samuel Baker. Is it possible they didn't notice the picture is missing?

'Tell the director I'll give him one last chance. I'll phone back in fifteen minutes.' Robert hangs up.

He thought of lots of things they might say when he phoned the gallery but he never expected them to altogether deny that the portrait of Samuel Baker had been stolen. Although come to think of it, as far as the gallery is concerned he is just a member of the general public. Why would they talk to him when they're trying to keep the story under wraps? He has to convince them he's the thief and that they won't get the picture back unless they negotiate with him. He leaves it fifteen minutes then tries again. This time a young lad called Tyrone answers the phone. Robert asks to speak to Evie. Tyrone says Evie is on her break. Robert explains he's already phoned twice this afternoon and left two messages and that this is the director's final chance.

'Ask him if he knows anything about a baseball cap and a scarf. You can put me on hold but don't cut me off.'

This tactic produces results. A few moments later a cautious voice introduces itself as the director and asks Robert who he is. As if he's going to tell them!

'We need to talk about Samuel and how you're going to get him back.' Robert is more confident now he has their attention. 'I have a price in mind and I warn you he doesn't come cheap.' Truth is, Robert hasn't a clue how much to ask. He's hoping the director will give him some idea of what would be reasonable. The catalogue says the artist who painted Samuel's portrait worked for King George III. You pay more for royal connections.

'Just one moment please.'

Silence. Surely the director hasn't cut him off?

'Hello? I think there's been a misunderstanding. If you're referring to John Riley's portrait of Samuel Baker, it's hanging on the wall of the Portrait Room. I've just been myself to check.'

It's Robert's turn to fall silent. This must be a bluff though the guy doesn't sound as if he is lying. Robert remembers clearly – third picture from the left on the middle row. William Craven, Bess of Hardwick, Samuel Baker. Bollocks! It depends which side of the door you're talking about. Samuel Baker hangs on the left of the door from inside the room, is it possible he counted three pictures in the middle row on the other side instead? He ends the call.

What an idiot! They'll never take him seriously now. They don't believe he's the thief. They think he's got wind of the story and is trying to make money on the back of it. The only way to persuade them to listen to him is to find out which picture he's actually stolen and that means going back to the graveyard.

Will –   *Can you believe it? The thief doesn't know which picture he stole! Apparently he intended to steal*

Samuel and took Hedova by mistake. The director was in here just now checking Samuel was okay.

Bess – What kind of thief makes a mistake like that?

Will – An inept one, I'd say. But such bad luck for Hedova. If the thief got it right she would be with us still.

Elizabeth – Does this have implications for how he'll treat Hedova? I mean if he didn't really want her in the first place?

Will – He'll take care she is not damaged. She's still a valuable commodity even if she is a mistake from his perspective. The crucial question is, will the director pay the ransom?

Elizabeth – He has a reputation for being tight-fisted. He won't pay a penny more than he has to.

Will – It all depends how long the thief is prepared to wait. If the director doesn't play ball the thief may try to sell her in another country.

Bess – Don't let Siegfried hear you say that.

Amy – Don't let Siegfried hear you say what?

Bess – Nothing for you to worry about, my dear. We were saying how well negotiations are going. Hedova will be back any day now.

Will – That's not an accurate representation of the facts …

Elizabeth – Shhhhhhhhh

Bess – Shhhhhhhh

Tia arranges the furniture in the Volunteers' Room so that it hides the worst of the carpet stains. She also covers the wobbly table with a hand-embroidered tablecloth and adds a little vase of flowers as a finishing touch. People are more likely to open up if they're in a pleasant environment.

They discuss how they'll conduct the interviews and agree Tia will get things started, then Douglas will take over while Tia records the evidence. They can both chip in if they think anything needs to be clarified or explored further. Before they begin Tia asks whether any of Douglas's friends in the Portrait Room have advice about investigating a theft. She's only teasing and doesn't expect an answer but of course he comes up with one.

'William was in effect the site manager responsible for the rebuilding of the West Wing at Coombe Abbey. I'm sure there was plenty of pilfering of tools and materials but I don't know how he dealt with it. William can certainly teach us a thing or two about perseverance though. The building work took forever to complete. He fought battle after battle with the architect, and the weather didn't help. But he ploughed on regardless. Felt it was his duty.' Douglas catches sight of Tia's expression. 'Are you laughing at me?'

'Not at you exactly, just at the way you always find a parallel in the life of someone from the Portrait Room.'

'It's become a major part of my life, that room. Therapeutic undoubtedly, but not obsessive, I hope.'

Hmmm. Tia suspects it's heading that way but who is going to tell him?

The first person to show up is the woman who heads up the publicity team for all the city's historic buildings, an exceptionally tall woman with purple hair, dressed in dungarees and chunky boots.

'I left a window open all night,' she confesses. 'The window nearest my desk. I was working late on Tuesday and didn't remember about the window till I was halfway home. By then I was so tired I simply couldn't summon up the energy to go back and close it. I know I should have gone back, and if it happens again that's what I'll do, but on Tuesday I was just too tired. If that helped the burglar, then I'm sorry.' Her voice takes on a defiant tone.

'Who said anything about a burglar?' Douglas asks.

'Come on! No one believes the cover story about *Head of a Girl* being sent away for research. A picture disappears from the Portrait Room and you ask us to tell you if we've noticed anything out of the ordinary. It doesn't take much imagination to guess what really happened.'

Tia asks if there's anyone she could have asked to pop in and close the window for her. The caretaker, for instance.

'It never occurred to me. I was so tired my brain had stopped working.'

Douglas asks if she saw anything to suggest someone had been in her office – furniture moved, muddy footprints.

'Nothing,' she says, 'not a thing. Do you think that's how the thief got the picture out? Let it down on a rope through the window to an accomplice waiting down below with a getaway car?'

Douglas advises her not to dwell on it. The windows don't open wide enough in any case. She goes away considerably more cheerful than when she arrived. Douglas closes the door behind her.

'I hadn't thought about a getaway car. Getting the picture out of the building is one thing, but he'd want to move it away from the area as quickly as he could.'

'That's true,' says Tia. 'I suppose there might be two of them working together. Or three, if we go for the insider theory.'

'I hope not. Somehow I feel we've a better chance of getting Hedova back if we're dealing with one individual.' Douglas stretches his arms wide and rotates his head a few times before getting back to business. 'Who's next?'

'The shop manager should be here any minute now.'

More than just a shop manager, as the gentleman is at pains to point out; he is in charge of all council merchandise marketing including online. It's pretty clear he bears a grudge against one member of his team and is glad of the opportunity to dish the dirt. He alleges the individual in question worked in tandem with the thief, fed him information and let him in and out of the building.

'What actual evidence do you have to substantiate your allegations?' Douglas asks.

'Nothing you could call hard evidence as such. It's more a case of instinct and intuition which, when it comes to solving crime, are every bit as valuable as what is normally classed as hard evidence.' The marketing manager reels off a long list of examples, citing specific police investigations and subsequent convictions. Fortunately, Douglas receives a call which brings the interview to a timely conclusion.

Tia gets up to stretch her legs.

Douglas comes back into the room. 'Anything useful?'

'Nothing. Nasty vindictive little man! Remind me to avoid him in future.'

'That was the director. The thief just made contact wanting to negotiate a ransom.'

'That's good news isn't it?'

'Not exactly. He wanted a ransom for Samuel Baker's portrait! Didn't mention Hedova.'

'That's very odd. He stole a picture without looking at it? I suppose you could make a mistake in the dark but you'd expect him to have a look once he got it home, at least before he phoned the gallery.'

'You'd think so.'

'What did the director say to him?'

'He told him Samuel's portrait is hanging in its proper place and the thief, if it was the thief, ended the call. We can't afford to upset him. He's our only hope of rescuing Hedova. If he takes the painting to a fence we'll never get it back and that's unthinkable. We just have to hope he makes contact again.'

The caretaker knocks the door. They listen as she repeats her story, smoothly and without hesitation. Too smoothly perhaps, as if she has prepared in advance. No, she doesn't check the stockroom every night – only when she feels like it and she didn't feel like it on Tuesday so she can't comment on the cap and scarf. No, she didn't see or hear anything unusual on Wednesday morning, not until she entered the Portrait Room. No, the alarm system hasn't been touched by anyone so far as she can tell and there is no sign of the doors being forced. The director has done a thorough check of the building, himself personally, and can't find anything suspicious.

Tia puts down her pen. 'Do you have any theories? I mean, how do you think he managed to steal the picture without being caught?'

The caretaker looks glum. 'I've been over it a thousand times and I can't for the life of me see how he did it. I guess he just got lucky and walked out with Hedova in broad daylight. He behaved as if he knew what he was doing so no one thought anything of it.'

When she's gone, Tia folds her arms and shivers. 'There's something not quite right about her. I have a feeling she knows more than she says. If it was an inside job, she's best placed to do it.'

'But that's circumstantial evidence. We don't have any independent reason to suspect her.'

Tia has to admit Douglas is right. They take a comfort break and return to find Julie from the café waiting by the door. She knows she's too early for her interview but she can't wait to get it off her chest.

'I don't know if this is the sort of thing you want to hear about, but you did say to come forward if we remember anything out of the ordinary.' Julie plays with her hair, winding it round her middle finger then tucking it behind her ear only to shake it free again a few minutes later.

Douglas reassures her that nothing is too small to mention and asks her to proceed.

'There was this man in the back corridor. He shouldn't have been there. Only staff are allowed in there, not members of the public.'

'Did you ask him what he was doing?'

'I didn't need to, that's the funny thing. He didn't apologise for being there. Came straight up to me and said he was looking for his son. He went to the toilet and never came back, his son that is, not the man. He thought his son might have gone into the staff corridor by mistake.'

Douglas wants to know if the man found his son.

'I offered to have a look but his wife texted to say it was okay. She said their son was feeling ill so she took him home. And the man said it was all right and pretended to smile.'

'Did you believe him? What he said about his son trying to find the toilet and his wife texting him, did you believe it was true?'

Julie considers this for a while. 'I thought it was odd when he said his son was sixteen. He didn't look old enough to have a son that age. At first he seemed to be talking about a young child. When I asked how old, he didn't answer immediately. Then he said his son was sixteen and autistic.'

Tia leans forward. 'You said he *pretended* to smile.'

'Did I?'

'Yes, just now. What made you say pretended?'

'It was an artificial smile. Like when you're being super polite. I didn't believe he was telling me the truth when I saw that smile.'

Tia asks if the man had a bag with him. Julie says no, he wasn't carrying anything.

'When was this? Which day?'

'Tuesday. No, Monday. That's right it was Monday. Soon after we finished serving lunch. I forgot all about it until we heard you wanted us to report unusual incidents.'

'Why didn't you tell someone at the time?'

Julie twists her hair furiously, tucking and untucking it at great speed. 'I should have but I didn't. Don't know why. I'll be in trouble for not telling, won't I?'

Douglas says he hopes not, the important thing is she's come forward now.

Tia and Douglas confer quietly, trying to contain their excitement. Is this the man who left the cap and scarf in the stockroom? It's possible he intended to steal the picture on Monday and Julie thwarted his plan. Or he may have been sussing out the building, working out how to get in and out without going through the main entrance. Douglas reminds Tia it's also quite possible the man has nothing at all to do with the theft, though instinct tells them he probably has. This is how it should be, Tia thinks, throwing yourself wholeheartedly into what you do and sharing that enthusiasm with your partner.

The first house she and her husband bought needed a new kitchen so they toured all the showrooms in the area and saw what was available. But when it came to making a decision about the colour of the unit doors, whether to have solid oak or marble worktops, the design on the tiles and the type of floor covering, she was disappointed. Instead of the negotiation and compromise she'd anticipated, Tia's husband told her she could have whatever she liked, and he made it sound as if he was doing her a kindness. She didn't want to choose by herself, she wanted him to be involved. People said she wore the trousers, and they were right, but it wasn't from choice; it was because her husband refused to put them on.

Douglas asks Julie whether she'd be able to recognise the man if she saw him again.

'I think so. I'm good with faces. He was fairly short and on the plump side. Light brown hair. Needs to change his barber.'

'I'll arrange for you to look through the CCTV camera footage from Monday,' Douglas says. 'See if you can pick him out.'

He makes the call. As it happens the engineer from the security company is in the area and can be at the Whitler in half an hour.

Julie begins messing with her hair again. 'I can't take any more time off. They need me in the café. It's half-term and we're already short-staffed.' A call to the café manager confirms what Julie said, they are very busy and can't afford to lose an able-bodied waitress.

Douglas has a solution. 'What if I cover Julie's shift? Not cooking or handling money, obviously, you need letters after your name to do that! But I can clear tables and deliver customers' meals. Then Tia can sit in with Julie while she watches the tapes.'

'Really? You'd be happy to do that?' Tia can't believe he's offering to fetch and carry other people's dirty plates and wasted food. He genuinely doesn't see any problem, in fact he seems pleased to do it. Fair enough. It's not Tia's place to stop him.

Julie goes off to buy herself some lunch. While Tia waits for the arrival of the engineer from the security company she phones Shompa. Bindu has been very quiet, Shompa says, but not unhappy. She's watched one video with the boys and now they're all going to the park to play on the swings and climbing apparatus.

'What's this all about, Tia? I thought you were on leave.'

'It's a bit hush-hush at the moment. I'll explain later. Are you okay to hold onto Bindu till I've finished? Another couple of hours perhaps?'

'No problem. She can sleep over if you like. But don't forget, when you pick her up I want a full account of your day.'

* * *

Robert pulls on a woollen hat. It soon gets cold these autumn nights and goodness knows how long it'll take to move the headstone. There's no lighting in the cemetery so he packs a torch in his rucksack along with the jemmy which he hopes will allow him to lever the headstone without further injury to his hands. It looks a tad suspicious going about with a jemmy in his bag but the chances of anyone searching him are zilch.

Robert stands at the bus stop, his rucksack slung casually over one shoulder. A young woman pushing a buggy hurries down the street and comes to a panting halt beside him.

'Have we missed it?'

Robert peers at the timetable. 'Hope not. It should be here any minute now.'

The child in the buggy, a little boy most likely though it's difficult to be certain, gives Robert a big grin. Robert smiles back. The child brings his hands up to cover his face and squints at Robert between his fingers, dislodging his dummy in the process. The woman, his mother presumably, is too busy texting to notice. The child begins to whimper. Without taking her eyes off the screen his mother reaches under the buggy's plastic cover and replaces the dummy between the child's lips.

Robert would like to have a child of his own, but he's not so keen on the idea of a live-in girlfriend, which is normally part of the deal. In his experience a live-in girlfriend leads to a clogged-up hoover and blocked waste outlets. All that brushing and combing and defoliating, and shaving legs and armpits and pubes, and plucking eyebrows, and removing facial hair. Trying to keep the house clean with all that going on would be even worse than clearing up after a dog. Perhaps one day, when he's properly established in his country cottage, he might go on a dating website and find a partner who shares his outlook and comes without all those unnecessary hairy extras.

The bus arrives. Robert helps the young woman lift the buggy on board, then he takes a seat towards the back. He still finds it difficult to believe he took the wrong picture. If it's true, his plans are totally messed up. He was supposed to start small with the portrait of a local man. If by mistake he's stolen something really valuable – a picture by some famous foreign geezer – the gallery may decide to call in the police and that'll put an end to any hope of making them pay a ransom. Robert will have nothing to show for his efforts, which feels much like the situation his dad often found himself in. Thinking of his dad reminds Robert why he's doing this. For excitement and adventure, yes, but also to find out what he's made of. This is the perfect opportunity; he's faced with a problem, let's see if he can keep his cool and sort it out.

When Robert came to the cemetery before – was it really only yesterday morning? – he went round to the rear entrance because he didn't want to be seen carrying the picture. Today he comes empty-handed and enters by the front gate. There is a small, unmanned building containing an exhibition tracing the history of the cemetery, and offering some guidance on how to pinpoint where your relatives are buried. He has a quick look then sets out to find the grave in which he hid the stolen picture.

Everything looks very different from this side and Robert can't get his bearings. He didn't write down any directions because he was sure he would recognise the spot, and anyway his dad taught him never to leave a paper trail. He remembers passing a boarded-up chapel but there's no sign of it from where he's standing. Then there was the group of fancy burial sites with marble angels and long inscriptions. And wasn't there a black marble tomb to the Oliver family close by? Yes, he's sure that was the name. Robert walks methodically from one side of the cemetery to the other keeping to the main paths, but he doesn't recognise any of it.

It's getting dark, almost too dark to read the writing on the headstones. He'll have to give up the search for tonight if he doesn't find the place soon. A distant howl sends a shiver through his bones though he knows very well it's dog not wolf. Robert has heard that after dark the cemetery is very popular with druggies and alkies, which may be an exaggeration but he isn't prepared to hang around long enough to find out. A low-flying bird swoops past his face, a swift, or could it be a bat? A wall topped with barbed wire cuts off his progress. Beyond the wall is a deep gully and at the bottom of the gully sits the railway line. Robert can't work out why the cemetery seems so different. Is the stress getting to him, making him confused? Come on! He can handle it. Tomorrow he'll find the picture and phone the poncey director and get him to pay through the nose.

Robert travels home on a bus crowded with teenagers on their way to a nightclub in the city centre. The girls make the most noise, screeching and snorting with laughter and exchanging obscene anecdotes in voices loud enough to travel from one end of the bus to the other. Egged on by her giggling friends, one of the girls sits beside Robert for a moment, deliberately pressing her thigh against his and fluttering her stick-on eyelashes in his face. He pretends not to notice but is acutely aware of his T-shirt soaking up the sweat.

* * *

Julie saw the man lurking in the staff corridor at around half past one so if they watch the tapes from half twelve onwards there's a good chance they'll catch him coming in through the main entrance. The security system engineer sets the tape rolling and leaves them to it and promises to hang around until they've finished.

Tia and Julie settle down side by side to eat their lunch while they squint at the too-small screen. Tia lifts her cottage cheese and avocado wrap out of its container and spreads kitchen paper over her knees to catch falling debris. Julie tucks into a generous portion of chips saturated with vinegar judging by the eye-watering smell, followed by a jumbo Mars bar. She can't fail to notice Tia's disapproval.

'I know, so bad for me but I don't do this every day,' she giggles. 'We all deserve a treat once in a while.'

This sounds to Tia very much like a variation of her husband's favourite plea but she refrains from comment.

It's a strange experience seeing people go about their everyday lives unaware they're being watched. Tia can't hear what they're saying but she doesn't need to, they give away so much about themselves by the way they walk and stand and move their heads and hands, the same gestures replicated a hundred times but with subtle differences. It's a very powerful tool. There's no arguing with the tapes, if they say it happened, it happened.

After a while Tia's mind begins to wander. She wonders how Douglas is getting on in the café and whether Bindu is brave enough to go on the climbing equipment. She has to keep bringing her attention back to the screen. Suddenly she sees something that propels her forward, bringing her face close to the images.

'That woman looks familiar. So does the little girl.'

Julie giggles. 'Of course they look familiar, it's you with your granddaughter!'

How stupid of Tia not to recognise herself! She has her hands on Bindu's shoulder as they come out of the café and walk past the main entrance on their way to the information stand. Bindu looks miserable and moody and it strikes Tia how much things have improved since then. Bindu has her moments of course but overall she's cheered up considerably and that's largely due to Douglas.

'It's hard on the eyes isn't it?' Julie presses her knuckles into her eye sockets. 'I have to screw mine up so as not to miss anything.'

They keep each other focused with the odd comment or joke as they continue to view the tape, but after one hour there's still no sign of the man they're looking for. Perhaps he wasn't an amateur after all, perhaps he knew how to avoid being picked up on CCTV. They decide to play the tape from the other camera, the one which is focussed on the information desk rather than the entrance. Tia goes to call the engineer and finds him sitting in his van surrounded by cigarette smoke which he tries to waft away as she approaches.

'Bad habit. I've cut right down. Promised my wife I'll quit altogether on my next birthday.'

Tia knows a thing or two about good intentions. 'Why wait till your birthday?'

The shame-faced engineer follows her inside. He removes the old tape and sets the new one running. Julie asks if he can make the picture clearer.

'Sorry. This is as good as it gets. The image isn't sharp enough to make a reliable identification. Wouldn't stand up in court.'

Tia records his comment in her notebook.

The view from this camera is more interesting. Evie and Tyrone are working their socks off attending to the queue of visitors at the information desk. They hand out leaflets and children's badges, direct visitors to the café, the toilets, the shop and the exhibitions as well as answering the phone. A demanding job which they do extremely well. If Tia owned a business she would employ them both without hesitating, which considering her standards is a huge compliment.

'I thought I knew what he looked like but seeing so many people confuses me.' Julie gives up punishing her hair and hones in on her bottom lip instead. Nibbling, sucking, puckering, pursing, picking – you name it she does it to her lower lip.

'Don't worry. You'll know when you see him. He must have come through the foyer at some point and I don't see how he could avoid the camera altogether.'

They've been watching for over an hour and Tia is about to suggest they take a break when Julie gives a little scream. 'That's him! Or someone who looks exactly like him.'

'Which one?'

'That one. At the front of the queue. I'm sure it's him.'

Tia rewinds and plays it through again.

'Yes! That's him. I can't see a wife and son with him, which they should be if his story is true. The lying bastard. Sixteen years old with severe autism, and I fell for it. I'm such a simpleton!' Julie groans. 'There's another thing. He pretended to get a text from his wife. Read it out to me. But you can't get a signal in the back corridor so he was definitely lying.'

Tia phones Douglas and tells him they've found the thief. He must have dropped everything and run, because a few minutes later he bursts into the Volunteers' Room. Together they stare at the face of the man they suspect stole Hedova.

'You'd never know would you, by looking at him? You wouldn't pick him out as a lawbreaker,' says Douglas thoughtfully.

'He fooled me,' Julie growls. 'I'd like to lock him up and throw away the key.'

Douglas points out that would be an invasion of his human rights.

'Can I go now?' Julie stands up. 'They must be struggling in the café.'

'Of course you can. Thanks for your help.'

Tia wonders where they go from here. They know what the suspect looks like but he is still only a suspect. They can't prove he was involved. And how does knowing what he looks like help them track him down? Unless they happen to bump into him walking down the road, which is possible but pretty unlikely.

Douglas wants to play the tape again to see if there are any clues, if they've missed something. They watch the sequence a couple more times. On the third go Douglas stops the tape midway.

'See that? Evie points to a sheet of paper and explains what it is. Then it looks as if our man writes something, takes out his wallet and pays. Let's see. Yes, she does the same with everyone in the queue but not everybody pays. We don't charge an entry fee so what's going on?'

For a moment Tia is afraid they're going to find evidence of a scam. Then with huge relief she exclaims, 'Raffle tickets! I remember now. Evie was selling tickets for the Children's Hospice raffle. She shows visitors the poster, asks if they would like to buy tickets and if they say yes she asks them to write their name and contact details on the ticket stub.'

'So we have his signature and contact details. That's brilliant! Find the right ticket and we've got him!' Douglas is exuberant.

Find the right ticket? How does he propose they do that?

Douglas goes off to see if Evie is free to come and look at the tape and show them the ticket stubs. Left by herself Tia plays the tape a few more times. Douglas returns with Evie. He's carrying a large box containing hundreds of ticket stubs. The Volunteers' Room is beginning to feel crowded.

'We can tell from the tape precisely when he bought the ticket but that's no good unless you've recorded on each stub the date and time you sold it.'

Evie confesses there is no way of telling when each ticket was sold, the thief's contact details could be written on the stub of any one of the five hundred or so tickets they've sold. She looks at the screen. 'I don't remember him. I see so many people and there's nothing special about him, is there?'

'I may be able to jog your memory. Look at this.' Tia plays the tape again then presses pause. 'Something different happens when our man buys a ticket. He's halfway through writing then he stops and you rummage in a drawer and pass him—'

Evie interrupts, 'A felt tip! The pen ran out of ink so I was trying to find something else for him to write with and that's all I could find.'

'I can see where this is leading.' Douglas can't keep still. 'Now this is important, Evie. Do you remember if the pen and the felt tip had the same colour ink?'

'They were different! I gave him a purple felt tip. It was the only thing I could find.'

'Excellent! So we need to find a ticket with the contact details starting off in black and ending up in purple. It won't take us too long if we share them out between us.'

No one speaks as they work through the piles of ticket books checking each individual stub. Suddenly Evie springs to her feet shouting, 'Got it! I've got it!' and punches the air. She holds the ticket up for Tia and Douglas to inspect. There it is, as plain as can be, the name in black, the phone number in purple. There's no room for doubt; this is the ticket bought by the man who Julie found lurking in the staff corridor. When they've calmed down they return the raffle tickets to the box and march together to the director's office.

Will –	Great news! They've had a breakthrough! They think they've found the thief.
Bess –	About time too.
Will –	That's unfair! It's only a few days since the burglary.

Bess –	Love can die within a few days.

Will –	That's not been my experience.

Elizabeth – Who are you referring to, Bess?

Bess –	Siegfried of course. Amy is doing such a good job of comforting him I'm afraid she'll steal his heart. When Hedova comes back she will find he's changed his allegiance.

Amy –	Slander! I'm not trying to steal him from Hedova. We offer each other mutual support, that's all.

Bess –	If you say so.

Will –	What would you say are the chances of Douglas and Tia getting together?

Bess –	I'd like them to. He's been alone long enough.

Amy –	Ugh! They're too old for that kind of thing.

Elizabeth – What kind of thing?

Amy –	You know what I mean.

Elizabeth – Don't listen to her. She doesn't know the first thing about love and even less about old age.

Bess –	You think you know about old age? You and Amy were painted one hundred and fifty years ago, three hundred years after you died! Will and I have been around for four hundred years. That's why Douglas talks to us not you. He knows we're genuine.

Will –	If Douglas and Tia do become an item she'll put a stop to his visits to the Portrait Room. I'll take bets on it.

Bess –	I do hope not. Life would be dull without Dougie to entertain us.

When Tia arrives breathless and apologetic it's Shompa's husband who answers the door. He's wearing a cookery apron and has a wooden spoon in one hand. He nods in the direction of the lounge. 'Go on through. She's enjoying herself, your Bindu, and the boys enjoy having her around.'

Tia finds Shompa sitting on the floor with the children. She's telling them a story, making it up as she goes along, putting on a different voice for each character. Currently she's a little boy clinging to the gunwale of his capsized boat while a storm rages round him. Bindu is so engrossed in the performance she doesn't notice Tia coming in, but Shompa does. She brings the story to a hurried end amid protests from her audience.

'Boys, can you help Bindu find her things?' Shompa closes the door.

Tia asks if Bindu has been okay.

'Never mind Bindu, how has your day been? What's so urgent that you had to cancel your annual leave?'

'Sorry Shompa, I can't tell you.'

Shompa frowns. 'Come on, Tia. This is Shompa. Your best friend.'

Tia puts her finger to her lips and shrugs.

'Give me a clue at least?'

'It's to do with the building. We are reviewing security procedures.'

Shompa bursts into laughter. After a moment Tia joins in.

'Okay, so you're not going to tell me. I'll just say this. You've been a lot more cheerful these last few days so whatever it is you're busy with must be doing you some good.'

Tia is brushing her teeth when Douglas phones. 'Bad news I'm afraid. The address on the raffle ticket doesn't exist and the phone number is invalid. It could be a genuine mistake but I doubt it.'

'No!' Tia is dismayed. 'After all those hours we spent looking at the tapes! I thought we'd nailed him. Hang on! What's the point in buying raffle tickets if no one can trace you? That's pretty dumb.

'I suspect he's not the brightest.'

'He must have done something wrong. Why would he give a false address if he was legit?'

'I can think of any number of reasons why a man might want to hide his identity. The truth is we are no closer to catching the thief than when we started.' Douglas is desolate.

'Come on, you're exaggerating! What about Julie's evidence?'

'We only have her word for it. And as you pointed out earlier, we still have no concrete evidence linking our man to Hedova's disappearance.'

Tia's heart aches to see him so miserable but there's nothing she can do about it.

* * *

Across the city leaves are changing colour in one final blaze of glory before they flutter to the ground; cherry red, corn gold, lemon yellow, peach pink, apricot, saffron, tangerine, honey, butterscotch, the flesh of a ripe watermelon plus a heap more mouth-watering shades. Leaves scuttle along pavements, swirl in alleyways, pile up in dark corners and nestle tight in long lines against the kerb. Stripped of their fiery finery the trees stand naked, warts and carbuncles exposed. Ever-widening pools of colour lap round their feet like the glowing embers of a lava flow.

Council workers remove sodden leaves from car parks, pavements and playgrounds; odd-job men unblock gutters and clear clogged drains. Keen gardeners head for the park armed with shovels and black plastic bags to gather leaves for their composting bins before park attendants hoover them up. Under instruction from their teachers, children stuff handfuls of their favourite leaves into their pockets to take to school for the autumn collage they're making.

Pale yellow leaves fall from the row of trees in front of Robert's flat. On the edge of the city Bindu looks out of her bedroom window and feels sorry for the prunus in her garden because its scarlet leaves are dying. She wonders if Hedova can see trees from wherever it is they have taken her. Half a mile away Tia and Douglas watch the caretaker clearing sludgy brown leaves from the steps leading up to the main entrance of the Whitler Gallery which is Hedova's rightful home. They would bring her back tomorrow if they only knew where to look. But they don't know because infuriatingly light travels in straight lines, and can't pass through solid objects, so they have to rely on their wits and not their eyesight to find her.

CHAPTER FIVE

It's the last day of half-term and Tia plans to drive out to the Whinnies, an area of natural woodland on the edge of the city, for a change of scenery and some fresh air.

Bindu pulls at Tia's sleeve. 'Can Douglas uncle come too?'

The idea has already crossed Tia's mind. She catches him before he leaves home.

'That's very kind of you but I should stay here, just in case he tries to get in touch.'

'You don't work on Fridays. Anyway, we're just down the road. If anything happens you can come back. Please do come, it'll take your mind off things. Bindu wants you to come.' Pause. 'So do I.'

'Okay. We all need cheering up. But you must let me drive. I'll pick you up in fifteen minutes.'

Douglas is a cautious driver to say the least. He maintains a speed at least ten mph below the limit and never overtakes even when they're stuck behind a tractor; exactly the opposite of the enthusiastic and passionate man he is when not behind the wheel. So the fifteen-minute drive takes almost half an hour during which Tia makes a superhuman effort not to criticise or comment. When Douglas has parked the car with admirable precision, exactly parallel to the only other car in sight, they head off through the timber kissing gate into the heart of the woods.

The Whinnies form a designated conservation area and are managed with a light touch, in other words left pretty much to look after itself. Light seeping through bare branches dapples the undergrowth and the habitual roar of traffic is replaced by birdsong. Underfoot the paths, composed of years of accumulated leaf mould, feel spongy. The area is a popular destination for families at weekends but this afternoon it's empty, except for the occasional dog walker and one young couple more interested in each other than the scenery.

Tia often brought her children here when they were young. They were living in an apartment at the time with no garden, taking them out into the countryside gave them the chance to get rid of some excess energy. Sometimes they took a picnic and stayed out all day. The children amused themselves and never complained of boredom.

'There's something reassuring about trees.' Tia runs her fingers across the deeply grooved and knotted bark of one exceptionally broad trunk. 'Just look at the size of this one; I can barely see the top. I wonder how old it is.'

Douglas comes to have a look. 'I don't know how old it is but those low branches make it good for climbing.'

To Tia's amazement he scrambles a little way up, straining to take his weight with his arms while searching for a firm foothold. He reaches a place where the trunk forks and makes himself comfortable.

'Bindu! Come and join me.'

'I'm scared.'

'Hang onto my hand and I'll pull you up.'

'Suppose I fall.'

Tia promises to catch her if she does but Bindu is ready with a list of other reasons for not climbing trees. It's clear she's not going to change her mind so Douglas descends, rather more quickly than he intended.

'It wasn't a very sensible thing to do. Look, what a mess I've made of my jacket.'

They walk on in companionable silence.

'I used to bring my wife here in the spring to see the bluebells. Imagine it. As far as you can see, the ground covered in blue!'

Tia says she's seen the bluebells and yes, they are wonderful.

'I haven't been here since she died. It seems like a betrayal. You know, I'm still here to enjoy it and she's not.'

'How long have you been on your own?'

'My wife died two years and three months ago. I was devastated. People told me it would gradually become more bearable and they were right. The bad days are just as bad as they were at the start, but they come less frequently and I've learnt how to manage them.'

'And you haven't found someone else, I mean a new partner?' In Tia's experience men pretty quickly find someone else.

'No. I think we were paired for life. Like George III and Queen Charlotte. At the time kings were expected to have a number of mistresses but not George. He adored Charlotte and died soon after she did, from a broken heart.'

So Douglas is still in love with his deceased wife, or thinks he is at any rate. That should mean Tia doesn't have to worry about him getting romantic ideas. But as everyone knows, people always insist they're never going to do the very thing they are on the verge of doing! For 'I stand by my minister' read 'I'll sack the bastard before the day's out.'

Tia senses Douglas is waiting for her to talk about her husband but is too much of a gentleman to probe. How can she explain what it's like to have your husband brought home each night, by his friends or random members of the public, too drunk to stand up let alone walk, or even worse not to come home at all; to wait for the phone call from the police to tell you they've found him lying in the street in a pool of his own vomit and piss and will you come and collect him from the station ASAP?

How can she explain what it's like to listen to the endless promises of new beginnings followed by fierce denials and finally an abject confession; to search your own house for bottles concealed behind the bath panel, in the attic, in the garden shed. The experience is neatly conveyed in a single paragraph but unspeakably sordid and messy to live through. Tia admits it openly, her husband's death came as a huge relief.

She says, 'My situation is very different from yours. It was not a happy marriage.'

A fallen beech tree blocks their way. Its tangled roots, torn out of the earth as it crashed to the forest floor, are exposed for all to see. Douglas sits astride one of its branches and bounces up and down as if it's a fairground ride.

'Do you want to try, Bindu? It's good fun!'

Bindu shakes her head.

'Tia?'

'Try stopping me!' Tia climbs onto the branch and bounces energetically. She begins to giggle and is soon laughing so much she has to ask Douglas to help her dismount before she falls off. Bindu looks embarrassed and walks on ahead.

'Did you hear someone phoned up wanting to know if we'd had a burglary?' Douglas makes a detour through a pile of fallen leaves, kicking up a shower with each step. 'Tyrone thought it might be someone from the *Gazette*.'

'No! How did they know?'

'I'm not sure they did know. Perhaps they read the notice about Hedova being sent off for research and smelt a rat. I think they were hoping to trick us into spilling the beans. Things don't look good as it is, if the press gets involved we have no hope.'

'Then we have to find the thief before they do.'

'Easily said.'

'Give me time and I'll think of something.'

Douglas smiles affectionately. 'You're right. We mustn't give up.'

There is a sudden flurry of movement and a burst of angry chittering. Bindu screams and takes refuge behind Douglas as two grey squirrels engage in fierce combat halfway up the trunk of a nearby tree.

'Don't be silly! They're not going to hurt you,' Tia scolds.

'They were trying to bite each other.' Bindu is on the verge of tears. 'Why do they do that?'

'I expect one is trespassing on the other one's territory,' Douglas says. 'Rather like humans, come to think of it. We wouldn't like strangers just walking into our homes whenever they felt like it.'

'My mummy brings people into our house and my daddy doesn't like it but he doesn't bite them.'

'I should hope not!' Tia manages a smile but feels unsettled. Who and what is Bindu referring to? Are Subir and Putul having problems with their marriage, and if so why hasn't Subir mentioned it to her?

* * *

Robert thanks the bus driver then crosses the road and follows the lane leading to the back entrance of the cemetery. This looks familiar. Yes, there's the boarded-up chapel emerging from the morning mist and near it the memorial to Sir Peter. Working outwards from there he spots the Oliver family's black marble affair. It takes another fifteen minutes trampling through nettles and brambles to find the grave he's looking for. So how come he couldn't find it yesterday? He walks along the boundary until his path is cut off by a wall topped with barbed wire, which is exactly what stopped his progress last night. Looking over the wall he sees the railway line and beyond that more graves. So the cemetery is split in two and last night he was in the wrong bit. He is not going mad after all!

Robert retraces his steps and gets to work on the tombstone. Using the jemmy as a lever he soon uncovers the picture. He slides it out, pulls back the bed sheet and reveals not the portrait of dumpy and plain Samuel Baker but the much smaller picture of a beautiful but sorrowful young girl. He sits a long while appreciating the girl's haunting beauty. The spiderweb shawl hanging off her pale shoulder; the dark hair parted in the centre and hanging down on each side of the sweetest ever heart-shaped face; the rosebud lips, pretty little nose and faraway eyes with a teardrop glistening on the lashes, all help make it an unforgettable picture. No need to take a photo, he'll have no difficulty picking her out of the Whitler catalogue. Robert feels he should apologise to the girl in the painting for snatching her from her cosy home in the gallery and leaving her in a cold and dirty graveyard. He wraps the picture up and slides it back into its hiding place.

Two elderly men appear from nowhere and walk towards him. Robert can feel his heart thumping and each breath is quick and shallow. He pretends to be clearing back the undergrowth round the grave. One of the gentlemen doffs his cap and says good morning.

'Come to pay your respects?'

Robert nods soberly.

'Who's in there, grandfather, great-grandfather?'

'Dad's dad. Died in the war.' Pillock! Why did he have to mention the war?

'Then how come he's buried here?' Both men peer at the tombstone. Fortunately for Robert the side bearing the inscription is underneath.

'When I say died in the war I mean died of his injuries after he came home. Shrapnel, travelled up to the brain.'

They bow their heads for a few moments and then move off.

Robert knows he should leave immediately but he can't move away from the grave so long as the picture is inside. He should have brought a plastic sheet. If it rains the paint and canvas will spoil and the picture will soon lose its value. And the temperature is wrong; when he was looking at the security system in the gallery he noticed each room has a separate thermostat. He doesn't know what temperature is ideal for this painting but none of the rooms in the gallery is as cold as it is outside in November. He simply must take the picture back to his flat. He'll hang it on the wall, may as well enjoy looking at it while he can. Only the mega-rich can afford to own pictures like this.

He drags the picture out again and moves towards the cemetery gate. Is it worth risking a bus? Someone might see him and be suspicious, or the driver might refuse to let him keep the picture on the seat beside him. He could phone Jamie and tell him the mirror is ready for collection and see if he is free, but Jamie hasn't been as friendly since Robert declined the offer of a ticket for the match. No, he'll have to carry it home, however heavy and awkward. He's thankful he didn't steal Samuel Baker, you would need a van to take him home.

It's a long haul. Robert is shattered by the time he reaches his block of flats and can't wait to get the picture safely inside. A woman with four boisterous kids is waiting for the lift. Robert tries to squeeze in beside them but the picture takes up too much room and he is forced to reverse out again. He waits another few minutes. Sod it! Just as he staggers out of the lift, Jamie opens his front door. This is exactly what Robert hoped to avoid. The last thing he wants is for Jamie to start asking questions.

'Hi there! Finished work on the mirror already? That was quick.' Jamie locks his door and follows Robert down the landing. 'You should have told me it was ready. I'd have given you a lift.'

'Thanks but they wanted rid of it straight away.' Robert has his key out, ready to nip inside quickly and avoid further conversation.

'Have they done a good job?' Jamie is close enough to pull the cover off the picture if he wants to. 'Can I have a look?'

'Not now, mate. Desperate for the loo.'

Robert's hand is shaking so much the key won't fit in the lock. He rests the picture on the floor for a moment and tries again. This time the key slides in smoothly and he opens the door. As he stoops to pick up the picture he inadvertently steps on the bedsheet, pulling it off one corner and exposing the frame and a small section of the girl's shoulder. He goes into his flat and quickly pulls the door to behind him then slides the picture under his bed – not a safe hiding place but at least it's warm and dry.

What exactly did Jamie see? Enough to make him suspicious, that's for sure. If he asks to see the mirror again, and he very likely will, Robert will have to come up with yet more lies. He doesn't know how long he can keep going without being caught out but for now he's going to hold his nerve. He's determined to get a decent ransom and to do that he must persuade the Whitler he's the person they have to do business with. He takes his trainers into the kitchen where he wipes and scrapes off the worst of the cemetery dirt. Then he settles down at the table with his laptop and a can.

Robert scrolls through the six hundred art works in the Whitler catalogue. How is he going to find the painting when he doesn't know the name of the artist nor the model who sat for him? Much of the gallery's stuff is fairly modern so he goes for the oldest and it doesn't take long to find her. There she is! *Head of a Girl* painted sometime between 1670 and 1720, they're not sure exactly.

The question is, what is she worth? She's either French or Italian and she's painted by a pupil of a well- known artist. That must make her ten times more valuable than Samuel Baker, the local boy made good. Robert feels a strange reluctance to put a price on the girl. She doesn't look as if she had much to call her own when she was alive; to put a price on this picture of her long after she's dead would be an insult. Don't be daft, Robert! Of course you have to put a price on her. That's what art thieves do. How else can they earn a living?

* * *

Douglas lifts one end of a decaying log and shows Bindu the numerous creepy crawlies hiding beneath it. He picks up a beetle with iridescent wings and places it on his palm where it sits a moment waving its legs before flying away. Bindu plods on eyes to the ground looking for beetles and wood lice and centipedes.

'She's a lovely little girl,' Douglas says. 'You should be proud of her.'

'Hmm.' Tia can't bring herself to agree but is reluctant to criticise a member of her family in front of an outsider.

Douglas senses she has reservations. 'Bindu's quiet and thoughtful,' he says, 'but that's not a bad thing, is it? We can't all be the life and soul of the party.'

'Some people never even get to the party! You have to make some effort.'

Tia's husband never made an effort. He would sit in his chair hour after hour doing crosswords and watching telly while she did everything that needed doing around the house and garden not to mention ferrying the children to and from their various activities. He would grudgingly agree to help if she insisted but he never volunteered, never took the initiative, never arranged an outing or booked a holiday. It strikes her for the first time she could be describing a future version of Bindu. Is that what she's afraid of, that Bindu will end up an alcoholic like her Thakuda?

'Bess of Hardwick had a favourite granddaughter, Arbella, whom she loved dearly. But things didn't work out well between them.'

'Why was that?'

'Bess was an ambitious and powerful woman. She wanted Arbella to be the same and found it hard to accept that she wasn't. Arbella was still sharing a bedroom with her grandmother when she was in her late twenties! Bess wouldn't give her the space to be herself.'

Tia glances at Douglas. Surely he's not comparing her with Bess of Hardwick? She points to a small bird perched high up on a twig and singing its heart out. 'That looks like a robin only its song sounds different.'

'Robins have one song for the spring when they're seeking a mate and another for the autumn when they're defending their territory.' Pursing his lips, Douglas delivers his version of the seasonal songs which Tia tries to imitate. 'They start singing at dawn, earlier than any other bird, and they go on singing until it's dark.'

Bindu lets out a shriek as she stumbles into a half-hidden stream. Tia hurries to her side. She's not hurt, thank God, only a little shaken and her socks are saturated. Tia pulls them off, wrings out the peaty water and puts them in her pocket.

'What about my trainers?'

'What about them?'

'They're wet too.'

'I can't do anything about that.'

'They feel horrible.'

'Sorry, darling, you'll have to put up with it unless you want to go barefoot.'

Bindu declares she has no intention of going barefoot.

They follow the little stream to the point where it widens into a pool and watch as sparkling fragments of light dance over the rippled surface. Bindu crouches down beside Douglas and puts her ear close to the stream so she can hear the music of water trickling over rocks.

'The woodland fairies come here to drink and wash their clothes when no one's around,' Douglas says.

'I know. I saw one.'

Douglas asks Bindu to describe it. Tia sighs. As if the child needs any encouragement.

When they reach the car park, Tia brushes dead leaves and twigs from Bindu's jeans. There's nothing she can do about the wet socks but there's no need to send her home with bits of the forest sticking to her.

That evening when Subir comes to collect her, Bindu rushes out to meet him. Tugging at his hand she says, 'Daddy, Daddy. Listen! I saw a fairy in the woods today. She was having a bath in a musical pool.'

As they are leaving Tia asks Subir in a whisper if he and Putul are okay.

He frowns. 'Why wouldn't we be? Why do you ask?'

'You're both in high-powered jobs. Loads of responsibility. It must be a strain.'

'It's been like that for ten years and you've only just noticed?' His irritation turns into amusement. 'Ah! Has Bindu been telling you about the lingerie ladies? Your daughter-in-law has signed up as an agent, goodness knows why. When they have their parties they fill the front room with lacy underwear and I'm banished upstairs to my study!'

* * *

Having identified the picture he actually stole, as opposed to the one he intended to steal, Robert is in a hurry to make contact with the gallery again. It's best if they don't realise he's the same person as the one who phoned yesterday. He needs another voice disguise, one that won't give him a sore throat this time. Posh perhaps? He's heard of people being trained to talk posh. They have to put something in their mouths while they talk, marbles isn't it? He doesn't have any marbles but an ice cube would make a good substitute. He takes the ice cube box out of the freezer and tries to eject one cube by applying pressure with his thumb. No luck. He bends the box backwards into an arch and the cubes shoot out across the lino. He scrabbles around on his hands and knees until he's retrieved them all, then rinses one under the tap and pops it in his mouth.

'Thank you for calling the Whitler Gallery. My name is Tyrone. How can I help you today?'

'Put me through to your director and don't ask any questions.' The ice is so cold it makes his teeth hurt.

'Pardon? Can you repeat that please?'

'I said, put me through to your director and don't ask any questions.'

'I'm sorry sir this seems to be a bad line. Did you say you wanted to ask a question?'

Robert spits the ice cube into the sink.

'Put me through to your director NOW!' He changes to a high squeaky voice which he hopes makes him sound like a woman, rather than a youngster whose balls haven't dropped.

'Can I ask what it's regarding?'

'Ask him if he wants to see *Head of a Girl* hanging on the wall again.'

'Please hold the line.' Tyrone's tone changes from patient to horrified. Perhaps he thinks Robert is threatening to cut off someone's head!

'Putting you through.'

Robert can hear the director's phone ringing. And ringing. And ringing. What's going on? Have they already told the police who are now trying to trace the call? Or perhaps they've put him on speaker so they can all listen to the wally who stole the wrong painting. That's it. They're having a good laugh at his expense.

'Good afternoon. This is the director. I understand you wish to speak to me.'

'We need to talk about *Head of a Girl*. I know where the picture is.'

'You mean you stole it.'

'That's correct, I stole it. But you can have it back for a price.'

'You want to sell my picture back to me?'

'Correct again. It's what art thieves do.' Surely the director's not that dim. 'I was thinking somewhere in the region of £50,000.'

Robert was planning to ask £25,000 but doubles it on the spur of the moment. The pundits say there's no way of fixing the value of a work of art; it's worth whatever someone is prepared to pay for it.

It suddenly occurs to Robert that he'll have to count the money, and do it on his own. Perhaps he should ask £25,000 after all, although even that is one hell of a lot of notes to work your way through, especially if the notes are those new slippery ones. Or perhaps he can count the money by weight like they do with coins? Though it wouldn't be very accurate; a £50 note weighs a fraction of a gram so he would never notice if a few were missing. Or he could measure the thickness of each pack of notes, though that would be even less accurate. He decides to ask to be paid by bank transfer, that way there's be no question of counting notes. Hang on, not a good idea. If he does that they'll be able to trace him.

'We need to settle on a sum acceptable to both sides,' says the director. '£50,000 is way too much. I suggest you come up with a much lower figure. I've been checking on other thefts of a similar nature to see how much ransom was paid. According to my research £10,000 is nearer the mark.'

The bastard! He knows the picture is worth far more than £10,000. He's stringing Robert along. Taking the mickey. 'I've told you how much I want and I'm sticking to it. If you're not interested I'll go elsewhere.'

That's the way to do it. Let them call his bluff and they'll see what he's made of. (Why do people say that? We already know what we're made of: flesh and bones and blood and hair and sixty per cent of it is water.)

'Of course we're interested. It's just a question of finding the right figure.'

Robert's anger at the paltry sum offered by the gallery is suddenly replaced by doubt and uncertainty. Supposing they refuse to pay and he's left in possession of the incriminating evidence. What would he do with the picture? He hasn't a clue how to go about finding a dealer to take it off his hands. Even if he does find someone prepared to buy it; what's to stop them reporting him to the police?

'Perhaps £50,000 is a bit steep. I might go down a smidgen. How would you feel about twenty grand?'

'I think I can persuade the board to give you £15,000 but that's the absolute limit.'

Robert is on familiar territory. He knows a thing or two about bargaining. He should do after all those antiques programmes he's watched.

He says, 'Let's split the difference and make it £17,500.'

Now that he's secured a deal, Robert has to work out exactly how the exchange is going to be made. He'll need a first-class disguise, none of your scarf and cap business. He can't risk being recognised.

CHAPTER SIX

The director spreads the large-scale map of the city centre across his desk and jabs at it with a jumbo marker pen. He is in what Douglas calls War Cabinet mode and the felt tip substitutes very nicely for Winston's cigar. Tia and Douglas stand one on either side of the commander-in-chief peering dutifully at the map and listening carefully as he warns them this operation has to be handled delicately. It's all very well to agree a price but that's only half the battle. The logistics of exchanging the picture for the agreed sum are complex and things could easily go wrong.

'Our thieving friend favours the little patch of grass at the back of the railway station as a drop-off and pickup point. God knows why. It's a place you'd steer clear of unless you're sleeping rough.'

'It does seem an odd choice,' Douglas jiggles the coins in his trouser pocket. 'Did he say exactly where we're supposed to leave the money?'

'In a litter bin. Just here.' The director jabs his pseudo-cigar at the small green triangle in the top left corner of the map.

Tia protests. 'A litter bin? Is that sensible?'

'Of course it's not sensible. Nothing this toerag does is sensible! But if he says leave the cash in a litter bin then that's what we have to do.'

'Okay. So you drop the cash in the bin and walk away. He comes to pick it up, I get that, but what next? How is he going to hand over the picture?'

'After he's counted the money, and that could take a while depending on how he does it, he'll put an envelope under this bench.' A sharp prod in the vicinity of the Peace Garden adjacent to the cathedral. 'The envelope will contain instructions about where to find *Head of a Girl*.'

Tia isn't convinced. 'How do we know we can trust him? What's to stop him walking away with the money and keeping Hedova just the same?'

'We can't be one hundred percent certain until we actually have the picture,' Douglas agrees. 'He could give us dud instructions.'

'It's the same for him though, isn't it? I mean he can't be sure we haven't given him forged notes until he tries spending them!' Tia is joking but the director spins round to face her.

'Now there's an idea! We can pay him in counterfeit currency.' Turning to Douglas. 'Any idea where I can get hold of £17,500 in forged notes?'

'I'm afraid not.' Douglas tries not to smile. 'Anyway, I'm not sure it's worth the risk. If he realises what we've done he won't trust us again and we'll never get Hedova back.'

The director straightens his back and thrusts out his oversized belly. 'Okay. So here's what you do. Douglas hangs around here, next to the taxi stand. Tia, you mix with the passengers standing in front of the departure board. Pretend to turn your bag inside out in search of your ticket or something like that. You'll see me drop the cash off, then make myself scarce. After that you must watch the bin like hawks. Thank God we already know what our man looks like; it makes things a lot easier.'

Douglas wants to know what they should do in the unlikely event that a member of the public picks up the bag.

'Tricky. We have to intervene but keep it low-key. Tell them you are plain-clothes cops and the bag contains highly sensitive material. That should be enough to put the wind up them.'

Tia bends over to study the map more carefully. 'Do you think he'll be alone? Won't he arrange for someone to keep a look out, warn him in case the police are lying in wait ready to pick him up?'

'Good point,' Douglas says. 'We should keep a look out for his lookouts!'

The director isn't amused. 'Like I said, it's a complex procedure and things could easily go wrong.' He tries clumsily to put the map away. Tia takes it from him, folds it neatly along the original creases and hands it back.

'When the thief comes to take the money, one of us follows him. Is that right?' She wants to make quite sure she has understood correctly.

'It is. I'll leave you to decide who does what. But don't try to talk to him and don't hang about. Just make a note of where he lives, then come straight back here.'

'And one of us goes over to the Peace Garden and waits for him to drop off the envelope?'

'Yes, but we're not sure when that'll happen. It depends if he wants to count every note individually before handing over the instructions.'

Back in the Volunteers' Room there's an atmosphere of anticipation. Shivers of excitement pass through Tia like bursts of electric current. She and Douglas exchange nervous smiles. This is the real thing, a genuine surveillance job!

'I'll tail him,' she says, 'I'm quicker than you.'

'I can't argue with that. But it's not only about being quick, is it? He could be dangerous. He could have a history of violence for all we know.'

Tia stands in front of Douglas, arms akimbo. 'There's another reason for me to do it.'

'How do you make that out?'

'He's less likely to hit a woman.'

'You have a naive faith in basic human decency!'

'Come on Douglas. I can look after myself.'

Once Tia has an idea in her head she's not easily deflected. She would love to be the one to discover who the thief is. Subir would be proud of her, and Bindu. And if she's honest Tia would also like to impress Douglas.

'Okay,' he says. 'I give in!' He buttons his coat up. 'Keep in touch. Let me know what's happening. And be careful.' For a moment she thinks he's going to give her a hug but at the last minute the hug becomes a good luck handshake.

* * *

The director promised to drop the money off in person and disappear immediately afterwards but Robert isn't sure if he can be trusted. Plain-clothes policemen could be waiting to arrest him, or the gallery might hire a private detective to follow him home. Robert can't take any risks. He needs a really good disguise, one that no one would ever imagine him wearing.

He peers through the shop window at the array of gorgeous outfits, mostly silk, embroidered in gold thread with sequins and tiny pretend pearls. The mannequins wear sparkly shoes and sparkly bangles to match. He can't see what he's looking for but that doesn't mean the shop doesn't sell them. Robert will have to go inside and ask. As he steps over the threshold all conversation ceases and all eyes watch him. He takes in the rolls of colourful cloth lining the walls and the rails of brightly coloured outfits. Perhaps they keep what he wants under the counter.

'Can I help you?' One of the shop assistants approaches him.

'I'm looking for one of those long black things women wear. The ones that cover you from head to foot. I forget the name.'

'Burqa?' She sounds surprised.

'That's the one!'

'I'm sorry. We don't sell burqas.'

Robert isn't going to be put off so easily. 'Do you know where I could get one?'

The shop assistant suggests it might be best to order one online. Robert doesn't have time for that. He needs a burqa by tomorrow. The assistant calls to the young woman standing at the head of the checkout queue.

'Aisha! Can you help this gentleman?'

'I can try.' Aisha finishes packing her purchases into a hand-stitched shopping bag, then jerks her head to indicate Robert is to follow.

Aisha leads Robert through a network of narrow streets, weaving in and out until he loses all sense of direction. They pass a series of little shops displaying vegetables and fruit Robert doesn't recognise and then turn left into a dark, damp passage running down between two houses until they reach the door of *Sultana Sewing*. A woman with a tape measure round her neck, a large pair of scissors clamped under her arm and two rows of pins stuck into her cuffs comes to the door. She and Aisha have a discussion in a language Robert recognises but doesn't understand.

Apparently *Sultana Sewing* specialises in making burqas to order, which is of no help to Robert who needs one today, but they also keeps samples for customers to try on for size and style. He's welcome to buy one of these if he likes. Robert says, yes please. He'd like to buy one of the samples. The sewing lady disappears leaving Robert and Aisha waiting awkwardly on the doorstep.

'Why do you want a burqa anyway?'

'It's for my sister. She's in a drama group. The next play they're putting on has an Arab woman in it.'

The seamstress reappears carrying a folded garment.

Aisha holds it up. 'What do you think? Will it fit her?'

Robert looks blank. 'Fit who?'

'Your sister.' Aisha frowns. 'Only a few minutes ago you said you want a burqa for your sister.'

'That's right. I do. But she's not going to wear it herself. It's her job to organise the costumes and props for the play.' Robert measures the garment against himself. It's roughly the right size. He'll have to practise walking in it without tripping on the hem.

'How much do I owe you?'

* * *

Tia sets off for the station on foot, trying not to look as if she's doing anything out of the ordinary. Douglas leaves a little later by another route. The director drives to the station car park with an orange carrier bag containing £17,500 in fresh notes stowed under the front passenger seat. It took him ages to persuade the bank manager he needed this sum, without revealing the true reason, at least not explicitly.

Tia takes up her position as instructed. The litter bin is visible from where she is standing but she can't see Douglas. She rummages through her bag for a while then consults her watch as if the person she's waiting for is late, then goes back to rummaging again. A familiar burly figure appears from the direction of the car park. The director! He saunters across to the patch of grass, pauses a few moments to catch his breath then casually drops the orange bag into the bin before wandering off again. A very credible performance. Now there is nothing for them to do but wait.

A train screeches to a halt before disgorging its cargo onto the platform. The stream of passengers divides to sweep past Tia and reforms behind her. She steps back and presses herself against the wall, surreptitiously studying the face of every man who passes by to see if it matches the face of the man on the CCTV footage. She's on edge and can't wait more than ten minutes before calling Douglas.

'How's it going?'

'I'm trying to merge into the background but it's not easy. People keep asking me directions.'

'Tell them you're a visitor yourself.'

'What, tell a lie? I couldn't do that.'

'Even if it helps us find Hedova?'

His answer is drowned by a change of platform announcement. For a while there is chaos as passengers gather their belongings and struggle up the stairs to cross the bridge or wait impatiently for the lift.

Tia catches sight of a dishevelled young woman heading for the little grassy patch. Tia crosses the forecourt, ready to intervene if necessary. Where's Douglas? Now she's closer, Tia sees the woman's jeans are in shreds, her hair is matted and there are sores round her mouth. This could be Bindu in ten years' time. Tia's stomach turns over at the thought. By nature and by choice Tia is an out-and-out optimist, except where Bindu is concerned.

The dishevelled woman stoops to pick up a cigarette stub and slips it into her pocket for later. She's on the move again and heading straight for the bin. *Where's Douglas?* Tia sidles a little closer. The director's orange carrier bag is clearly visible but the woman doesn't touch it. She fishes underneath, rescues a half-eaten sandwich and half a banana still in its skin and wanders off to find somewhere quiet to eat them. Tia returns to her position in front of the departure board.

'Where were you?'

'Sorry. I needed the toilet. Weak bladder. Did I miss something?'

Tia can't control her laughter, and soon Douglas is laughing too.

A woman wearing full burqa wanders over to the little patch of grass. She lowers herself wearily onto the bench and sits there, knees splayed and head resting in her hands.

Another ten minutes pass without incident. You'd think the thief would be keen to get his hands on the money.

Tia looks at the clock on the departure board. She's dying for her mid-morning boost of caffeine. The woman in the burqa eats a bar of chocolate and goes over to put the wrapper in the bin. Douglas notices her and moves closer, cautiously, not wanting to interfere unless it's necessary. The woman reaches into the litter bin and withdraws the orange bag. Douglas strides towards her, pointing at her hand and shouting. The woman drops the bag, picks up the hem of the burqa so it doesn't slow her down, and sprints off down a side street. Passengers stand open-mouthed and watch her go. By the time Tia arrives it's too late to give chase.

'That was him, wasn't it?' she gasps.

'Must have been.' Douglas is in a state of shock. 'How else could she – I mean he – know about the bag?'

Tia is furious with herself. 'I should have guessed he'd come in disguise.'

'That doesn't matter now. The point is we promised not to hang around. We broke our promise and he's never going to trust us again.' Douglas looks so miserable Tia can barely resist the urge to throw her arms around him. 'You realise this means there's very little chance of Hedova ever coming home?'

* * *

When he's certain he's not being followed, Robert slows to a normal pace. The bastards! They agreed not to watch out for him. He was quite clear about that; they were to put the money in an orange carrier bag, place it in the litter bin, and go away. He really thought they'd do it. Now he knows they can't be trusted, he's never going to do business with them again.

So what is he going to do with the picture? He has to get rid of it soon, before someone reports the theft to the police. Robert has to admit, the possibility of being caught really spooks him. Yesterday when he walked past the building which serves as a combined Crown and County Court, he saw prison vans queueing up to carry their human cargo down to the car park underground. The van windows were blacked out but he caught a glimpse of the profile of one particularly vicious-looking passenger. It struck him with full force – he's been behaving as if stealing the picture is a game. It isn't. He really could be sent down for what he's done.

He knows what life inside is like. He's heard the technicolour version from his dad. The screws deliberately losing your mail and blocking visits from your family, and demanding protection money then turning a blind eye when other prisoners beat you up. The drug dealing and intimidation and bullying and forced sex. Cooped up in a cell for twenty-three hours a day with a violent criminal.

Robert turns left into the park, checks no one's watching then disappears behind the toilet block. Watched by a grey squirrel, he hauls the burqa over his head, stuffs it into the hedge and re-emerges as himself.

Jamie suspects something's going on. If the word gets out that a picture has been stolen he'll put two and two together and go straight to the police. And God knows how many other people saw him struggling home with the picture yesterday. Mr and Mrs Stokes and Zelda for sure. Sometimes he feels they are all spying on him. Robert has a sudden crazy vision of the police surrounding his flat with armed officers and calling him out with one of those loud speaker things. Forget about being brave, forget about the ransom, call it cowardice if you like, he doesn't care. He only knows he has to return the picture to the gallery as soon as possible.

When he gets home, Robert drags *Head of a Girl* out from under the bed. He wraps it in layers of newspaper secured with sticky tape, then adds a string handle to make it easier to carry. His plan is to abandon the picture where it will be easily found. To make sure it finds its way back to the right place he writes out a label saying "Property of Whitler Gallery. Please return to owner ASAP" and fixes it to the package with sticky tape.

He pulls on his woolly hat, grabs his jacket. Trying to hold the picture in a way that won't attract attention, and keeping the side with the label next to his body, he sets off towards the city centre. He can remember taking the same route a week ago, and thinking how dull and bored everyone seemed. Strange, today the people he passes look relaxed and content. It begins to rain. Not good for the picture. He pops into a corner shop to buy a roll of garden refuse sacks then tries to slip a couple of them over the picture, one from each end. A middle-aged couple stand and watch.

'Need any help with that, mate?'

'I'm okay thanks. Found this in the attic. They're doing evaluations for free today so I thought I'd take it along.'

Pillock! Why did he say that? He hasn't even got an attic! And suppose they ask the address where he's taking it to be valued, what will he say?

'Good luck!' the woman says under her breath.

'I hope it's a lost masterpiece and you get millions for it,' the man jokes.

Robert picks up the picture and, with a nod to the couple, makes his way to the Lower Precinct where shoppers tend to gather when it's raining. A rough sleeper emerges from his sleeping bag to find the world and his wife tramping through his bedroom. A busker sits cross-legged and plays Vivaldi hoping shoppers will toss coins into the violin case lying open in front of him. Skateboarders thunder down the ramp from the council house, leap onto the wall surrounding the fountain, turn one hundred and eighty degrees, mid-flight, and shudder to a halt by the main entrance to the library. Plenty to distract attention from Robert which is just what he needs.

There's a sprinkling of benches, most of them occupied by wrinklies. Sliding the picture under the seat, Robert squeezes in-between two gentlemen, one with his nose buried in the tabloid press the other sharing his opinions on the political issues of the day with anyone prepared to stop and listen. Robert sits a while watching the pigeons and the occasional seagull make the most of half-eaten sandwiches and discarded tortilla wraps. Pretending to answer his mobile, Robert gets to his feet and heads off towards the library. He doesn't get far before the man with the surfeit of political opinions cups his hands and bellows after him.

'What about the parcel? Going to leave it here are you?' He reaches under the seat. 'Good thing one of us is awake!'

Robert hurries back, thanks the man and grabs the picture before anyone notices the label. Bugger! Try again.

He climbs the stairs to the library and enters the non-fiction zone. He props the picture up against one of the book stacks, halfway down the aisle so it's not visible from the central area, and begins to browse the alphabetically arranged shelves, slowly moving further and further away from where he started. Philosophy, Politics, Religion, Science, Sociology. He's been there ten minutes and he's fairly sure no one has noticed his partially concealed package. It should be safe to make his exit now. As he leaves, the young woman on the enquiry desk smiles and thanks him for coming. He's halfway down the stairs when he hears footsteps behind him and someone touches his arm.

'I think you forgot this, sir. It does belong to you, doesn't it?' A disgruntled library assistant hands him the picture.

Once again Robert pretends to be very grateful. 'Thanks. How could I forget? You'd think it was too big to lose.'

Now what? He could try leaving it on the steps of the gallery or maybe in the forecourt but someone is bound to see him; he may as well give himself up and have done with it. Thoroughly disheartened Robert drags himself and his cargo back to his block of flats. He tries not to look at the miserable, pathetic face staring at him out of the mirror as the lift carries him higher and higher. If only it would continue for ever, up beyond the moon, beyond the sun, never reaching its destination. No such luck! The doors slide open when they reach Robert's floor.

As he emerges, old man Stokes waves at him from the other end of the landing but there's no sign of Jamie, thank God. Robert is turning his key in the lock when he notices Zelda standing quietly in front of one of the pictures hanging on the wall. There's nothing special about it, it's just one of the silver-framed, mass-produced prints found in hotels and offices. She's not interested in the picture, she's actually waiting for him.

'What you got there, Sonny?'

'A painting. By my great-grandfather. He was an artist.' Why did he say that? Suppose Zelda and Jamie compare notes. Safer to stick to the mirror story. 'Well it's actually a picture with a mirror in the middle. Or you could say a mirror with a picture round the edge.'

'This I must see!'

'Not just now, Zelda. I'm knackered. Some other time.' Robert disappears into his flat and locks the door. Sod it. He's offended her. If they come looking for him now, she'll be the first to dob him in.

CHAPTER SEVEN

Tia is in the garden with the pruning shears when Douglas phones. She knows this isn't the best time to prune but she can't stand the unsightly mass of overgrown shrubs and bushes any longer. According to the gardening programme the cut ends are susceptible to rot in the damp and cold of November, that's why she is taking care to cut the stalks at an angle so when it rains the water runs off.

Her father understood plants. Leaving his wife and children behind he came to England to study gastroenterology and was desperately homesick. His landlord offered him the use of an empty greenhouse at the end of the garden so he filled it with vegetable plants to remind him of home; bitter gourds with an abundance of yeast-scented yellow flowers, broad flat Bengali beans, varieties of *shak* (one with red stems, another which at home climbed up the walls and covered the roof of his father's house), chilli peppers of all shapes and sizes, and a plant with sour red flowers which he sweetened and turned into a refreshing drink or *chatni* – chutney. When, at the end of his course, Tia's father was offered a consultant's position in a large teaching hospital, he sent for his family to join him. Although he was no longer homesick, he continued to grow vegetables.

Tia wishes she had taken more interest. But at the time she was doing her utmost to fit in with the girls in her class, tossing aside anything which marked her out as different. She and her siblings refused to eat the rice and dal and curried fish their mother prepared, preferring to stuff themselves with fish and chips and sausages in batter (even Tia couldn't bring herself to break the ultimate taboo and eat a beefburger).

By the time Tia removes her gardening shoes and gloves and locates her mobile, Douglas has rung off. He leaves a message asking her to return his call. She wonders if there's been some new development. Perhaps the thief has contacted the director offering them another chance to get Hedova back. Douglas answers immediately as if he is waiting for her to phone.

'The board has demanded to see the director first thing Monday morning. They heard what happened at the station. They want a progress report.'

'We haven't made any progress.'

'If we admit that they'll insist we go to the police. He wants to give them something positive to be going on with. That's why I'm phoning. He wants to meet with us to discuss it.'

'When?'

'He's suggesting Sunday morning.'

'But we don't open on Sundays.'

'Precisely. He's looking for a suitable venue.'

'I'd be very happy for you to come here.' She wonders whether to make blueberry muffins or carrot cake, then comes up with a better idea. 'If you like you can stay on after the director leaves and we can continue our discussion over lunch.'

'That's very kind but I'm not easy to feed. I'm gluten-intolerant. I'm also allergic to nuts and when I tried sprinkling turmeric on my breakfast cereal as advised by the assistant in the health food store – don't try it by the way, it tastes revolting – I came out in a rash.'

'I have a shoulder of lamb in the freezer. I was planning to do a Sunday roast à la Delia with all the trimmings.'

'Just the ticket! Thank you.'

'See you tomorrow at eleven.'

Tia changes out of her gardening gear and gets to work on the house. It is good to have a motive to clean and tidy the place, although it never gets really dirty, not with only one person living in it. She checks her supply of ground coffee. She can pop over to the supermarket later for a carton of cream. Better take the meat out of the freezer now before she forgets.

She's quite excited by the thought of cooking for Douglas. The relationship between two people changes once they've eaten each other's food. No two people like their food prepared in exactly the same way so there's bound to be some disappointment but if they do like what you've cooked it gives you enormous satisfaction.

Tia has a very clear memory of the first time she and her husband cooked for each other. It was a few weeks before their marriage. He invited her round to his student lodgings where she made *luchi* and he made *chholar* dal. Her *luchi* were perfect, light and flaky and not at all oily in spite of being deep-fried, he couldn't deny that. But when he asked how she liked his dal she told him it was tasty but needed to boil for longer and could do with a little more salt. This was quite true but he couldn't take such direct criticism from her, or anyone else, and went off in a huff. When she tackled him about it later, asking if he'd rather she pretended there was nothing wrong when there patently was, he ignored her and walked away. And he continued to walk away from anything which required negotiation and compromise for the remaining thirty years of their marriage.

The director arrives twenty minutes early. Fortunately, Tia has everything under control. She offers him a seat but he's restless and is soon on his feet again. He wanders round Tia's front room picking up one object after another, asking how she acquired it and claiming he's got one just like it at home. The spherical silver box where Tia's mother kept her jewellery, the little fish carved from Whitby jet Tia bought for herself last summer, the tiny replica of the Eiffel Tower made entirely of matchsticks. He's full of bluff and bluster and Tia has to make an effort to be polite. It's a relief when Douglas shows up, exactly on time. Tia serves coffee then takes out her notebook and they get down to business.

The director goes through the evidence and summarises the current state of affairs, which they all admit is not good. They're still a long way off proving the man in the CCTV tape is the thief.

'Any idea how we can move this investigation forward? I have to give them some hope.' The question is directed at Douglas but it is Tia who replies.

'I have a plan which just might work. We can pretend one of the tickets he, the thief, bought won the Hospice raffle and that so far no one has come forward to claim the prize. We'll advertise the ticket number and ask people to check if it's theirs. It's quite a generous pot of money, he might be greedy enough to come and collect it.'

Douglas is right behind Tia's proposal. 'Excellent! We can pay out the prize money and then when he leaves, one of us tails him.'

The director is sceptical. 'Haven't you already tried that?'

'We'll be better prepared this time.'

'And how is our thief going to discover the winning ticket hasn't been claimed?'

'Publicity. I haven't worked out the details yet. Douglas will help with that.' Tia looks over at Douglas. 'He knows people in high places!'

'Do I?' Douglas is taken aback.

'I meant you have contacts with the local press and radio.'

The director shrugs. 'I suppose it's worth a try. We've got nothing else and he might just be stupid enough to fall for it. Judging by his phone calls he doesn't have much between his ears.'

Tia remembers the figure in the burqa and feels an unexpected twinge of sympathy. They're setting a trap and he's going to walk straight into it. *Jah*! What's wrong with her? He's a thief and thieves belong behind bars.

'I suspect the board will instruct me to inform the police. I'll try to stall them while you put your idea into practice. The more background info you can supply, the more likely the police are to take action.'

They've finished the meeting but the director shows no sign of moving. Tia repeatedly studies her watch. Isn't someone cooking him Sunday lunch? It's another twenty minutes before he takes the hint and gets to his feet.

The instant the director departs the mood changes. If the atmosphere was navy blue while he was with them now it's the colour of a summer sky; if it was bottle green before, now it's the first leaves of spring. Douglas sets the table while Tia makes gravy. He carries the serving dishes to the table while she fills a cut crystal jug with iced water. She sharpens the carving knife while he fetches the mint sauce which she made yesterday and almost forgot about. Everything they do is punctuated by laughter. It feels to Tia suspiciously like flirtatious laughter; on the other hand it might be the laughter of friends who share a common purpose.

'This is an excellent meal.'

'Thank you, glad you're enjoying it.' Tia carves a few more slices of lamb and lifts them onto Douglas's plate. 'We can ask the person with the winning ticket to report to the information desk within three days. We can take turns watching out for him.'

'And when he turns up—'

'*When* not *if*?' Tia is surprised at his confidence.

'I'm pretty sure he'll turn up. He won't be able to resist.'

They polish off just about everything on the table, except the parsnips which are tough and woody, and adjourn to the front room where they are working their way through a box of liqueur chocolates when a blue car with a sun roof swings into the drive.

'You have visitors,' Douglas declares. 'I'll be on my way.'

'Stay right where you are.' Tia means it to be a request but it sounds like a command so she adds, 'I'd really like you to meet my son if you can spare the time.'

Subir climbs out of his car and goes round to open Bindu's door, as if she can't do it perfectly well herself, and a few minutes later they appear in Tia's front room. (Subir insists on having his own key in case Tia can't get to the door for whatever reason.)

'Sorry, bad timing. Bindu wanted to come and see you. I didn't know you had company.' Subir looks from Tia to Douglas and back with surprise and amusement.

'You wanted to see me?' Tia holds out her arms. Bindu comes towards her, sees Douglas, hesitates then changes direction, ending up in the seat on the far side of Douglas. Tia pretends not to notice.

'Pleased to meet you, Douglas.' Subir sticks out his hand. 'You've made quite an impression. She enjoyed the Whinnies so much she wanted to go again. We spent yesterday afternoon there.' He looks over at Tia. 'It hasn't changed much. You used to take us when we were kids, remember? To get us away from Baba.'

Tia wonders if he realised this at the time or only in retrospect.

Subir and Douglas launch into a discussion on the preservation of the natural environment, especially with regard to insects. Douglas describes how years ago the windscreen and bonnet would be thick with dead insects after a long journey. Subir listens with genuine interest. They are a good match. Tia allows herself to imagine Douglas joining the family for birthday celebrations and taking part in the festivals of Durga and Saraswati.

She reaches out and touches Bindu's hand. 'Your daddy said you wanted to see me. Is there something you want to say?'

Bindu picks at the skin round her fingernails for a moment. Looking at her father she says, 'I wanted to say thank you for looking after me.'

She's only doing what she's told, Tia thinks. She doesn't mean it. 'No need to thank me. I enjoyed having you.' Tia's not sure if she means it either.

Before she goes to bed that night Tia takes down the small red leather suitcase which sits on the top of her wardrobe, and leafs through the pile of school reports, prizes, certificates and newspaper cuttings it contains. Underneath the papers she finds Subir's first pairs of shoes, a tiny pillow filled with mustard seeds, her daughter's half-size sari for dressing up in and a stainless steel *jhinook*, much more efficient at guiding liquid into a baby's mouth than an ordinary teaspoon.

Her heart melts as she recalls the pleasure she took from bathing and breastfeeding and rocking her children to sleep. The feel of her children squirming in her lap with all the wiry energy of a landed fish, or fast asleep with their bodies moulded to the contours of Tia's body and not a hair's breadth to separate them. She used to love it when her children were too sick to go to school. An excuse to indulge them with cuddles and strokes and massage.

But why did she need an excuse? Why did she feel the need to ration the meeting of skin with skin? Tia's own childhood was surrounded by touch at every turn; she shared a bed with her sisters, three of them in a row their limbs so entwined you couldn't say whose was which. And for the first few years of her marriage there was plenty of touching, both passionate and tender. But it didn't last. Once her husband had explored her body he seemed to lose interest and she was too proud to take the lead and risk being rebuffed.

Who touches her now? Subir from time to time but not too often and only if Putul isn't watching. Tia and her friends hug each other but rarely does the embrace last more than a few moments or have any weight to it.

* * *

Robert normally does a couple of rounds of Whitler Park on a Sunday morning to stretch his legs, then buys a paper from the corner shop on the way home; but today he stays inside. Instead of doing the puzzles page and reading Letters to the Editor he watches horror movies. He likes horror films but this morning they don't hold his attention, his mind keeps wandering off. At midday Robert opens a tin of soup which he eats with the tail end of a stale bread roll, followed by an overripe banana for dessert. He is used to a proper Sunday dinner but he would rather make do with what there is in the flat than go to the shops in broad daylight and have someone recognise him as the man who stole the picture from the Whitler. To all intents and purposes he is a prisoner in his own home.

Having struggled all morning to keep awake so as not to miss any of the action, Robert now stretches out on the sofa for his customary Sunday afternoon snooze. The sound of his own snoring wakes him a couple of hours later. Robert keeps his eyes tight shut and tries to convince himself it's all a nightmare, that his mind is playing tricks and he never really stole the picture. But when he opens them again he knows it is all true, there really is a chance he'll go to prison.

Robert goes into the bathroom. Hoping to release some tension he takes one of the men's magazines from the pile in the airing cupboard and props it up on top of the cistern. It doesn't help. Afterwards he splashes cold water on his face and brushes his teeth with his electric toothbrush.

His only hope is to make the evidence disappear. You can't accuse someone of theft if there is no stolen property in the same way that you can't have a murder trial without a body, well only in exceptional circumstances. Tomorrow he'll tell the gallery they've lost their chance, he's sending the picture abroad. Then with any luck they'll leave him alone and put their energy into searching harbours and airports. But right now he's hungry.

It's almost dark. He'll slip out and buy something more filling than soup for his evening meal. He pulls down his woolly hat until it touches his eyebrows, winds a scarf round his neck and over his mouth and turns up the collar of his jacket so that most of his face is hidden. He opens and closes his front door as quietly as possible and tiptoes towards the staircase. He's never liked the colour of the carpet on the landing but today he's grateful to it for muffling his footsteps. He reaches the main entrance without anyone seeing him. So far so good.

The big supermarkets close early on Sunday but there's a branch about a mile away which stays open till late. Robert decides to walk rather than take the bus, to make up for missing his morning round of the park. The road cuts through a newly built private estate, rows of pretty houses with neatly paved front yards for off-road parking and shrubs in glazed china pots on either side of the front door. Thick curtains blank out the windows so Robert can't see inside but he can imagine the homely scene, mum and dad and two kids packing rucksacks and briefcases ready for a fresh week at school and the office.

He can see one of his bleak, lonely moods heading in from the south pole. His mum and dad were rubbish parents but at least they were relatives. Now they've both gone there's no one he can call family, no one who knew him as a baby and shares his bloodline. His mum's sister, Aunty Kath, was driven into an early grave by a strict and bloody-minded husband and his dad's sister, Aunty Beryl, spent her life pulling pints in smoky pubs and died young of lung cancer. For God's sake Robert, don't start feeling sorry for yourself! You've got a roof over your head and money in your pocket. Well, you have at the moment anyway, if the director of the gallery goes to the police all that could change.

As he reaches the other side of the housing estate Robert hears footsteps coming up behind and turns to see who is following him. The street is empty. He moves forward a few hundred yards and again hears footsteps. This time when he turns round he sees a figure slip silently behind a tree. Have they put a tail on him or is his brain playing tricks from lack of food? He's heard of starving people having hallucinations.

This is just the kind of situation he thought he would enjoy until he tried it. Now he knows it's not his thing at all. He hesitates; the quickest way is over the footbridge which isn't normally a problem but if someone is following him he'd rather be on solid ground. He takes the longer route and is relieved when at last he reaches the safety of the store.

Robert takes a basket and makes straight for the ready meals. Lamb or beef? He can't decide so he takes one of each. He'll put one of them in the freezer; on the other hand he's so hungry he might eat them both. He's tempted by the tiramisu. Why not? He needs cheering up. He's moving down the aisle in the direction of the bread counter when someone rams a trolley into him from behind. It feels as if it was done on purpose but before he can get a good look, whoever did it disappears into the wines and spirits section. Robert rolls down his sock and examines the broken skin on the back of his left heel. If someone is trying to frighten him they're making a good job of it. He grabs a box of teabags and a carton of milk and hurries to the checkout.

Robert wonders what he's capable of if it gets physical. For instance what will he do if he hears someone is grassing on him? Cut out their tongue of course! But the tongue is an awkward little bugger, slippery and muscular and difficult to grab hold of; he'd need to secure it with a bent paper clip pushed through the tip and keep it stretched while he cuts through the muscle. Or if he couldn't manage the tongue he could slash the traitor's cheeks so the words escaped through the slits. A few months ago Robert acquired a meat cleaver in exchange for loyalty points in the supermarket. The cleaver stays in the kitchen drawer doing nothing; it would be good to see it put to use chopping a body up into manageable pieces. And the hacksaw would make short work of the bones. Question: would a new tongue grow in place of the old one? Question: would his victim bleed to death? There, that wasn't so bad was it? It's left him feeling nauseous but he's proved he can look violence straight in the eye.

Of course it's all nonsense; he would never actually do any of it. Just think what a mess it would make! All that blood and liquid fat and bile seeping into the carpet. And they say the anal sphincter relaxes when you die so there would be a load of shit to clean up along with the blood and other bodily fluids.

The woman who joins the queue after him says something to her partner. Her voice sounds exactly like Evie's, the woman who answers the phone when he calls the gallery. Robert doesn't want to look at her in case she recognises him but he's absolutely certain it is Evie or her twin sister. When it's his turn to go through the checkout Robert pretends he can't speak. He carries out the transaction with signs in case Evie recognises his voice and raises the alarm. By the time he comes out into the cold and damp, he's too shaky to walk home so he phones for a taxi.

Robert only manages to eat half of his lamb dinner before crashing out on the sofa; he can't face sleeping in his own bed knowing *Head of a Girl* is lying under it.

* * *

Douglas drives home in reflective mood. It's a very long time since he found another person's company so pleasurable, so rewarding. Tia knows how to handle herself. She was unfailingly polite to the director although it's clear she doesn't much like him. And when Bindu chose to sit next to him, Douglas, instead of next to her, Tia showed no reaction although he's certain she was hurt. Like William, Tia knows how to live in the world without being dragged down by it. She is absolutely not the sort to indulge in self-pity or navel gazing, she's more likely to get up and do what she can to improve her own lot.

And what a charming house with its cheerful clutter of ornaments and pictures. A collection of etchings by coal miners, bought during a trip to Northumberland, because Tia admired the men for sticking to their mining roots and combining manual labour with artistic skill. Hanging on the wall opposite the etchings was a poster advertising a Bollywood film next door to a lavishly decorated programme for a cultural event celebrating the festival of the goddess Saraswati. What surprised Douglas most was the collection of soft toys in the downstairs toilet, which somehow managed to be cute without being twee.

She'd treated him like one of the family rather than a guest. Had even accepted his offer to help with the washing-up so long as he stuck strictly to her four-step regime; remove leftovers, wash thoroughly, rinse, leave in the rack to dry! Germ-laden tea towels are banned.

Douglas suspected she might be strict about her diet and hesitated before buying chocolates in case she considered them unhealthy. Far from it. She picked out her favourites and put them in a little pile which she kept all to herself! At first he was a little taken aback when she kicked off her sandals and tucked her legs under her, but on reflection he took it as a compliment that she was so utterly relaxed and informal in his presence.

Douglas longs to confide in Will and Bess, to tell them how having such a lovely time at Tia's house has left him crippled with guilt and regret. For a while he allowed himself to entertain feelings of tenderness and warmth towards a woman other than his wife, something he never expected to happen. Is he being too harsh on himself? Douglas conjures up the portrait of Siegfried. The hero stands naked in the middle of a fast-flowing river, one foot placed triumphantly on the crumpled body of the scaly beast he has just slain, one hand gripping the sword he used to execute the deed. The lad's head is thrown back and he appears to be looking at the giant bird hovering in the top right-hand corner of the picture, as if this is the next enemy to be vanquished. But close up you can see Siegfried's eyelids are actually lowered in grief. Perhaps Douglas has framed the question wrongly. It isn't a case of either honouring his dead wife's memory or finding someone new; it's possible to do both side by side. In fact he has no choice but to do both, to remember the dead and celebrate the living.

CHAPTER EIGHT

'Listen up! You remember we told you about the raffle the Whitler Gallery is running in aid of the Children's Hospice? First prize £500. Well, guess what, no one's claimed the winning ticket! Turn out your pockets, look in your bins, down the back of the sofa, under the bed. You're looking for ticket number one hundred and seventy-seven. So get treasure hunting all of you. Good luck and don't forget to phone in and tell us if you find it! Now over to Anna for the weather. Hi Anna, how long is this rainy spell going to last?'

Jamie is finishing his brunch when he hears the appeal for the holder of raffle ticket number one hundred and seventy-seven to make contact with the Whitler Gallery. He bought a couple of tickets on Tuesday, or was it Wednesday? He didn't buy them because he felt sorry for the children – although of course he does – and he didn't buy them to win the prize money – although of course he wouldn't say no to £500. He bought the tickets from the woman on the charity stall in the market because he fancied her! Couldn't take his eyes off her. Hair down to her waist, huge eyes, and leggings so tight you could practically see the stitching on her thong.

Jamie searches his jacket and his jeans, then grabs the car keys and bounces down the stairs to the little patch of concrete where his car is parked. Nothing in the ashtrays or the side pockets. He rummages through the rubbish on the floor. Handouts, lecture notes, leaflets and flyers, and yes, a crumpled set of raffle tickets. A strip of six. He recognises the Whitler Gallery logo but he doesn't remember buying that many. Must have been hoping to impress the goddess who was selling them! What number did they say to look out for? He's forgotten already. He takes the lift back up to his flat and spreads the crumpled tickets out on the table in front of him while he checks the gallery website.

'Thank you for calling the Whitler Gallery. My name is Evie. How can I help you today?'

'Morning Evie, my name is Jamie. Can you confirm the number of the ticket that won first prize in the raffle?'

'We are looking for the owner of ticket number one hundred and seventy-seven.'

'I've got it. I'm looking at it right now!'

Pause.

'Congratulations!'

'What do I do now? I mean how do I claim the prize?'

'Can you bring the ticket down to the gallery? We are open until four this afternoon.'

'I'll come down right away. Who shall I ask for?'

'Ask for Evie. That's me. I'll be on the information desk.'

She asks a colleague to cover for her then heads off to the Volunteers' Room where she finds Douglas listening intently while Tia makes a case for the caretaker being hand in hand with the thief.

'We've got him!'

Tia looks up from her notebook where she's recording her argument. 'Got who?'

'Him! The thief. He's just phoned. He has ticket number one hundred and seventy-seven.'

'That was quick! It's only an hour since we asked the radio station to run the story,' Douglas says.

'I told him to bring the ticket down here. Is that right? What do you want me to say to him when he arrives?'

Douglas looks at Tia. 'Well done! This raffle ticket trap was your idea.'

'Well done to you too. You were convinced he'd turn up. I wasn't so sure.'

'I'd better go and talk to the director.' Douglas gets to his feet. 'Can you stay with Evie in the foyer?'

'Okay.' Tia slides her notebook into her bag. 'But don't be too long. If we make him hang around he'll get suspicious.'

Evie and Tia hurry back to the foyer where Evie resumes her position behind the information desk and Tia pretends to be studying one of the leaflets while keeping a close eye on the door. She conjures up the face of the stout middle-aged man who stole poor Bindu's favourite painting, one of the few things Bindu is passionate about.

Douglas returns from his audience with the director, has a quick word with Tia then installs himself near the entrance to the shop where he has a good view of the entrance. Half an hour later there is still no sign of the thief. Tia moves closer to the window so she can see right into the street. Someone touches her arm making her jump. She looks round to see Evie accompanied by a tall gangly lad with ginger hair straggling over his collar.

Evie says, 'This gentleman has ticket number one hundred and seventy-seven. Could you take him to see the director please?'

Tia can't believe what her eyes are telling her. For a few moments she's too flummoxed to speak. This isn't the man from the CCTV tape. There's been some kind of mix-up. Douglas strides over and rescues her.

'Congratulations! We're delighted you found the ticket.'

Jamie grins. 'Not half as delighted as I am!'

'If you'd like to come this way we'll just do the necessary paperwork.' Douglas leads the way to the director's office. Tia, having recovered from her shock, chats cheerfully to Jamie as they follow. He tells her he's a second-year psychology student and that he plans to stay on to do an MSc in criminology. Tia can't work out what's going on. This can't be the person who stole Hedova and is negotiating a ransom, he seems far too relaxed; nor is he the man on the CCTV and yet he holds the winning ticket.

The director's face registers surprise followed by suspicion as his PA ushers Douglas, Tia and Jamie into his office. He is as confused by Jamie's appearance as the rest of them are. He invites them to sit. His manner is polite and formal. He doesn't take his eyes off Jamie and he doesn't smile.

'I gather congratulations are in order. You're the lucky winner of five hundred pounds! Before I hand over the prize money I need to run a few checks. May I?' The director takes the ticket Jamie holds out to him. 'Shouldn't take long. To start with, can you tell us your name please?'

'Jamie. Jamie Fletcher.'

Long pause. Change to a more hostile tone. 'I'm afraid that's not the name we have against this ticket.'

Jamie laughs. 'You're joking, right?'

'Unfortunately, not. This ticket was bought by someone calling himself Pete. We have CCTV footage of Pete buying the ticket and he doesn't look a bit like you. How do you explain that?'

'I can't explain it. I only know I bought some raffle tickets from the charity stall in the market and one of them was the winning number so I came in here to collect the prize.'

'I think your memory is playing tricks on you or to put it more bluntly I think you're telling porkies. I think a friend of yours gave you this ticket and asked you to claim the prize money in his name and on his behalf.' The director leans forward and stares intently at Jamie across his desk. 'I'm right aren't I?'

'Look, what's going on exactly? You're treating me like I've committed a crime.' Jamie goes to pick his ticket up but the director is too quick for him.

'I'll keep that for now. How about telling me the truth? I think you know very well why your friend didn't collect the prize money himself. He wants to keep a low profile, doesn't he? He knows he'll be recognised if he comes in person so he sends you to collect it for him.'

Jamie gets to his feet. 'I don't have to put up with this. Forget the frigging prize money. I'll see myself out.'

'If you try to leave, I'll call the police and accuse you of fraud and of being implicated in theft. As I think you know very well, someone stole a picture from our gallery, a valuable one, and we suspect you are involved.'

Tia is on her feet too. Surely it's obvious to anyone with

an ounce of intelligence that Jamie isn't the thief or in league with the thief. He's a run-of-the-mill student who happens to be in the wrong place at the wrong time. It often happens, an unfortunate set of circumstances make a person look guilty when in fact they aren't.

'I believe he's telling the truth.' She smiles at Jamie. 'Why would he tell us his name is Jamie if he knew the name on the ticket was Pete? Somehow the tickets have got muddled up. That doesn't mean Jamie's done anything wrong.'

She resumes her seat and Jamie follows her example.

'To be honest I was surprised to find six tickets,' he says. 'I thought I only bought two. But if these aren't my tickets,' he shuffles uncomfortably, 'then how come they were lying on the floor of my car?'

Douglas suggests someone dropped them there when Jamie gave them a lift. 'Have you had anyone in the back seat of your car recently?' Jamie giggles. Douglas looks embarrassed and rephrases the question. 'Can you remember who you've given a lift to in the last few days?'

'I've taken friends out a couple of times. No one called Pete though.'

'You're wasting your time.' The director is getting impatient. 'He's Pete's sidekick, it's obvious. Why are you two working so hard to get him off the hook?'

Douglas says, 'Because we have to give him the chance to prove his innocence. Jamie, can you phone the friends who have been in your car recently? Ask if they've lost any raffle tickets.'

Jamie reluctantly makes the calls. The others converse in whispers and pretend not to be listening. None of Jamie's friends admits to buying tickets let alone losing them. This particular line of enquiry seems to have reached a dead end. Then Jamie remembers.

'There was someone. My neighbour. Wednesday morning, early. Just out here on the road behind the gallery. He said his uncle's mirror needed restoring. A large antique mirror with a fancy frame, he said, though I didn't see it myself. I gave him a lift. Dropped him off near the cemetery on South Road. I don't have his phone number but when I get home I can pop round and ask whether he's lost any raffle tickets.'

Stunned silence. The three of them share a single thought. The director is the first to recover. 'What does he look like, this neighbour of yours?'

'Not very tall, stocky. Recently changed his hairstyle. Close shave. Doesn't suit him.'

'And you gave him a lift on Wednesday?' The director again.

Jamie nods. 'My neighbour, yes. I wouldn't call Robert a friend exactly.'

Tia says, 'And you say he was carrying a large, framed mirror?'

'He told me it was a mirror. Only later, on Friday, when he brought it back to his flat the cover slipped off one corner and it didn't look much like a mirror.'

'He brought it back to his flat?' Tia echoes him lamely.

It's too good to be true. This is precisely what they need. A link between the man who bought ticket one hundred and seventy-seven and was found by Julie lurking in the corridor, and the man who walked away with *Head of a Girl*, in the guise of a mirror as they now know.

'Is it in his house right now?'

'In his flat. I guess so. His uncle left it to him in his will. Robert was close to his uncle.'

'He calls himself Robert does he? Robert what?' The director reaches for his pen.

'I don't know his surname.'

'Of course you don't!' under his breath.

Jamie says, 'You don't think Robert is into theft, do you? I'd be surprised. He's a quiet guy. Keeps himself to himself. Wouldn't have the balls to do anything illegal.'

'We'll be the judge of that,' the director snaps. He turns to Douglas. 'What do you think? Are you prepared to go and check it out?'

'I'll go and see what's what, if Jamie points me in the right direction.'

'Points *us*,' Tia says. 'I'm going with you. Two opinions are better than one.'

'I'd rather you stayed here.' Douglas looks to the director for support but doesn't get it.

'Tia is right. Better stick together. There's no risk of aggression or violence is there, Jamie?'

Jamie shakes his head. 'Not that I know of. Like I said he's a quiet guy. Friendly enough but prefers his own company.'

The phone rings. The director ignores it. It continues ringing. He lifts the receiver.

'I said no interruptions. Ah! Right. I see.' He waves his free hand peremptorily to indicate they should all leave the room. 'Yes, you can put him through.'

Tia watches the director through the glass screen. He says nothing for a while but she can tell by his clenched jaw and frown that he doesn't like what he's hearing. Now he's doing the talking, gesticulating forcefully, trying to persuade whoever is at the other end to do or not to do something. Douglas isn't watching, he stands at a polite distance, hands in pockets, rocking back on his heels, reading the flyers and leaflets pinned to the noticeboard. Jamie is busy with his mobile, his thumbs dart across the screen. The director slams the receiver down, startling Tia and bringing Douglas to her side. He beckons through the glass, calling them back in.

'The bastard's changed his tune. He's sending our picture abroad. It might be a bluff but then again he might be serious.'

'Then we have to stop him. We have to rescue Hedova.' Tia is already half out of the door. She's doing this for Bindu, she hadn't realised it before. 'Are you coming Douglas? Jamie?'

Douglas offers to drive but, remembering the painfully slow journey to the Whinnies, Tia insists on taking her car. Jamie hops into the back while Douglas climbs in beside Tia. He doesn't have much leg room so Tia shows him, with rising impatience, how to slide his seat back. They're losing precious time. She revs the engine and screeches out onto the main road before the others finish doing up their belts. They pass through lights on amber and don't stop for hesitant pedestrians, only for those who have actually set foot on the crossing. They bypass congested highways by weaving their way through narrow side streets and twice they execute an illegal U-turn on a dual carriageway. Jamie asks whether Tia has ever considered a career in Formula One.

Douglas rests a hand on the dashboard, bracing himself for yet another vicious jolt as Tia brings the car to an abrupt halt in front of a relatively well-kept block of flats. Each flat has its own balcony stuffed full of potted shrubs with variegated leaves and berries, alongside items of garden furniture wrapped in plastic waiting for the spring. Tia urges them to hurry. Robert could be booking his flight at this very moment, one seat for himself and one for the picture. (Surely he wouldn't trust something so valuable to the luggage hold?) Tia and Jamie head for the stairs while Douglas waits for the lift out of consideration for his knees. He arrives on floor 6 a few seconds before they do.

'That's Robert's flat. With the doormat outside.' Jamie points to a door halfway down the landing.

'How do you want to do this?' Douglas asks.

'I'll go and have a word,' Tia says. 'You two wait here. I can say I'm doing a survey on behalf of the Whitler. Show him my badge. I'll bring the conversation round to the Portrait Room and see where that leads us. I might even squeeze a confession out of him.'

Douglas tries to persuade her to swap tasks, he will knock on the door and she will wait outside. 'Certainly not,' she says. 'Men don't feel threatened by women, whereas a man confronting another man is an open invitation to use force.'

'That may be so in general but at this particular moment you look remarkably threatening,' Douglas says rather timidly. 'I wouldn't like to cross swords with you.'

She laughs. 'If I don't reappear within an hour, come and find me.'

'One hour is too long.' Douglas is uncharacteristically tense.

'Okay let's make it forty-five minutes. Not before.'

'No heroics?'

'No heroics. I promise.'

* * *

'Listen up! You remember we told you about the raffle Whitler Gallery is running in aid of the Children's Hospice? First prize £500. Well, guess what, no one's claimed the winning ticket! Turn out your pockets, look in your bins, down the back of the sofa, under the bed. You're looking for ticket number one hundred and seventy-seven. So, get treasure hunting all of you. Good luck and don't forget to phone in and tell us if you find it! Now over to Anna for the weather. Hi Anna, how long is this cold spell going to last?'

Robert remembers buying a strip of six tickets last Monday. He checks the left side pocket of his jacket. Nothing. That's odd, he's sure he put the tickets there, it's where he keeps all his till receipts and other important scraps of paper. The tickets must have fallen out. Possibly when he took out his wallet to pay for the meal on Wednesday evening. No, he was wearing his smart jacket on Wednesday. On the bus going to the cemetery and back? No, he paid his fare with small change from the jar beside the sink. At the off-licence? He hasn't been to the off-licence since last Saturday and he bought the tickets on Monday afternoon so that wouldn't work. Wednesday morning in Jamie's car? That's it! Everything spilled onto the floor when he took out his wallet to make a contribution towards petrol. He remembers picking up the receipts, but he must have left the tickets on the floor. Not to worry. The way his luck is going he's sure he didn't have the winning number.

Robert takes his coffee to the table and tries to work out precisely how he is going to get rid of the painting. There is a half-empty tin of white gloss in the cupboard in the hall. He could paint over the girl's face with that, but suppose somebody got suspicious and scraped it off and found the girl's face still there looking out at them, frightened as hell, from underneath the white gloss?

He could burn her but that would set off the smoke alarm, unless he lit a bonfire in the park. And it would look suspicious having a bonfire all by himself. People would ask questions. If the flat had a garden he would bury the picture, really deep so no one would find it for a hundred years. But his flat doesn't have a garden. Here's what he'll do. He'll cut the girl into tiny pieces so small they can't be recognised and put them in the wheelie bin. Not all at once, a handful each week.

Robert turns the picture face down on the living room floor and crouches beside it. The backing is made from poor-quality timber and should be easy to take apart. At some point a couple of labels have been stuck on the back. He can't make any sense of the numbers and letters but he knows, from watching antiques programmes, that they can be useful if you want to know which auction houses have handled the purchase and sale.

He turns the picture face up again. The frame looks as old as the painting, which is rare according to the online article he read. Usually the owner changed the frame when he bought a painting, to make it fit in with the style of his other possessions. This frame seems to be made from a single piece of wood, at least Robert can't find any joins. It's carved all over in the form of grapes and flowers and has been gilded in the past but most of the paint has flaked off. It should be easy enough to saw it into little pieces with his hacksaw, carefully so no one hears him. But not until he's finished cutting up the picture. The canvas has to be stretched taut in the frame so he can cut it with his blade.

Robert goes to the cupboard in the hall, takes out his Stanley knife, his hacksaw and a handful of spare blades for each, and places them on the glass-topped table. He swallows the last mouthful of coffee, places his mug in the sink and fills it with soapy water so as to prevent stains. Now he's ready to begin. He slides the knife blade forward and tests the sharpness on the corner of the frame. Not good enough. He wants a clean cut; he owes it to the girl and to the artist to do the job properly. He discards the old blade and fits a new one. He plays with the knife, extending and retracting the blade trying to buy time before slicing into the girl's tearful face.

It's almost a relief when the doorbell rings. Robert peers through the spyhole. A woman. Fundraising? Trying to persuade him to set up a direct debit for £2.00 a month (surely the admin costs outweigh the income) for disadvantaged dogs/cats/donkeys/children? Robert puts the knife down. Sliding the picture out of sight under the settee, he goes to open the front door.

* * *

The first thing to strike Tia when the door opens is the smell. Bleach, disinfectant, cheap air freshener and sickly floral fabric conditioner combine to make her eyes smart. Perhaps that accounts for the redness around Robert's eyes. Either that or he's been crying. There is no doubt about it, he is the man she saw on CCTV, but close up in real life he doesn't look in the least bit like a criminal, in fact he looks more like a victim.

'Good afternoon. My name is Tia and I'm from the Whitler Gallery.'

Robert thinks she looks vaguely familiar.

'We're carrying out a random survey to gather opinions from the public about how we should develop our services. You've been chosen to take part. Could you spare the time to answer a few questions? It shouldn't take more than twenty minutes.' Tia shows Robert her badge and gives him what she hopes is a cheerful, non-threatening smile. It works! He leads her into the front room and invites her to take a seat. Robert sinks into the settee beside her. She gets the impression he's pleased to have company. She doesn't feel the least bit afraid.

'This is a nice flat! How long have you lived here?'

'Nine years eleven months. But I don't expect to be here much longer.'

'Oh?'

'I've been offered a job in Saudi Arabia. I fly out next week.'

Interesting! Does he plan to get rid of the picture before leaving or take it with him and sell it to a wealthy sheikh? Although to be honest Tia doesn't think he looks like someone about to leave the country to work abroad.

'Shall we get started?' She searches in her bag, makes a joke about being low tech unlike today's youngsters, and pulls out her notepad and pen. 'Can you tell me roughly how many times you've visited the Whitler during the past year?'

'I'm down there most weekends. As it happens I was there three days running last week.'

If this is true, surely the staff would know him? 'We'll go into specifics in a minute but overall, on a scale of one to ten, how would you rate your most recent visit?'

Robert considers this carefully. The meal was good and the ground-floor exhibition wasn't bad but sleeping on the floor between two cupboards wasn't much fun and stealing the painting was pretty stressful. 'Somewhere between four and five,' he says.

'I'm sorry to hear that. We aim for a score of eight or above. Do you have any suggestions as to how we could improve?'

That's a tricky one. Getting out of the building was the most difficult part by far but he can't very well suggest they take the keypad off the back door. 'Pass,' he says.

'Okay. Let me know if anything comes to mind. Next question, did you find the staff friendly and helpful?'

The waitress was genuinely concerned about his imaginary son. She deserves a nine at least. But supposing Tia asks why he gives her such a high score, what's he going to say? A mid-range answer would be best. 'I can't complain. Then again I didn't need help.'

'Did you find the information given alongside each exhibit useful?'

'Oh yes. Definitely. You wouldn't understand the pictures without it, would you?'

'Is there any picture you actually dislike? We like to know our patrons' tastes. It helps when considering future acquisitions.'

Robert doesn't want to answer that. Apart from *Head of a Girl* the only other picture he can recall is the portrait of Samuel Baker and he can't choose that without raising suspicion. He shakes his head. 'No. Not really. What about you? Do you have a favourite or aren't you allowed to say?'

She's tempted to say *Head of a Girl* by a pupil of Furini and see how he reacts. 'I love all the pictures in the Portrait Room. You must know it.'

Robert shakes his head. 'Nope. I stick to the ground floor. Don't like heights.'

'But…' She turns towards the window.

'I know. I live on the sixth floor. Torture. I never used to mind. My fear of heights came on recently. That's why I'm moving out.' He gets to his feet. 'Would you like some tea?'

'Thank you. My throat gets very dry doing these interviews.'

Tia gives herself a pat on the back. She has him eating out of her hand! She has a quick look round while he's out of the room. The furniture and decoration have nothing distinctive about them, you could find the same in millions of homes across the country. Although the huge pink flowers on the curtains are a bit overpowering, especially when paired with a red carpet! There's a collection of cactus plants, and a couple of framed photos but no other individual touches.

If only she could find the picture. Where would he hide it? She simply has to take a look. If he comes back she can pretend she suffers from cramp. She strolls casually out of the room and turns left towards the kitchen. The door of the room adjacent to the lounge, a bedroom probably, is slightly ajar. She peers through the gap but the curtains are drawn and it's too dark to see inside. She is on the point of investigating further when she hears a door close. He's coming back! Tia resumes her seat just as he enters the room. In her haste she drops her pen. While she's scrabbling around under the settee her fingers brush against something soft, a piece of cloth, and inside the cloth there's something straight-edged and solid. Could it be…? No! Surely he wouldn't leave it in such an obvious place.

'If you could just shift your legs to this side a bit.' Dropping to his hands and knees Robert retrieves the pen and passes it to her.

Tia keeps the interview going for a further twenty minutes. She chooses questions which give him the chance to talk about himself and he grasps the opportunity. By the time she's finished they're chatting away like old friends. She picks up one of the framed photographs.

'Is this you?'

He nods. 'Taken on my tenth birthday. That's my mum.'

The woman's blouse is at least two sizes too big and her hair's a mess. She throws her arm round her son but her eyes are focussed on the book lying beside her on the sofa. It's obvious the minute the photo shoot is over she'll pick up the book and start reading from where she left off. Behind her, Robert's dad breaks off a conversation with his drinking mates just long enough to lay his hand on Robert's head and smile at the camera. Robert himself looks out at the photographer with stoic resignation. His expression weighed down by responsibilities is better suited to the face of a middle-aged man than a ten-year-old kid.

'That's about it, I think. Thank you so much for your cooperation.' Tia puts her notebook and pen back in her bag. 'Is there anything you want to ask me?'

'I can't think of anything.' He's despondent. He doesn't want her to leave. 'Will you let me know the results of your survey?'

'Certainly. I'll add your name to the distribution list.' She slips on her coat. 'Oh, by the way, have you heard about the missing raffle ticket? There's a prize of £500 waiting to be claimed.'

'They mentioned it on the radio just before you came. I bought some tickets but I haven't a clue where I put them. Looked everywhere. They must have fallen out of my pocket when a friend gave me a lift.'

Making a big effort to keep her voice steady Tia says, 'We think the winning ticket was sold sometime on Tuesday.'

'I bought mine on Tuesday, or was it Monday? Anyway it was before Wednesday because that's when my friend gave me a lift.'

Robert doesn't realise it but he's just handed Tia the victory. He's verified Jamie's story and by his own admission put himself in the right time and place to commit the theft. With directness and no emotion Tia says, 'I think I can guess what you were carrying when Jamie gave you a lift. And it wasn't a mirror was it?'

At first Robert looks bewildered; he's wondering how Tia knows his friend is called Jamie. Then the truth dawns, the whole survey thing is a trap! He is furious. His face turns puce as he thrusts his fist into Tia's face, stopping only a few centimetres clear of her jaw.

She stands her ground. 'Listen Robert, we know you're a thief. We know it was you who stole *Head of a Girl* from the Whitler Gallery. We've collected enough evidence to convict you. But if you hand the picture to me now I promise we won't involve the police.'

'You think I'm going to believe that?' between clenched teeth.

Tia could point out that Robert doesn't have a choice, that she's not alone and any minute now the others will come to rescue her, but that would back him into a corner and a cornered beast is very dangerous.

Robert grabs the Stanley knife from the glass-topped table. Tia doesn't believe for one moment that he'll use it on her. As if he's come to the same conclusion, Robert drops to his knees in front of the settee and hauls the picture from its hiding place. Globules of sweat form on his forehead as he presses the tip of the blade into the canvas. Tia is sick with fear. Surely he won't destroy such a valuable and precious object?

To take the heat out of the situation she says, 'My granddaughter loves that picture. She's been miserable since it disappeared from the gallery. She made a print of it to put on her bedroom wall. She'll be terribly upset if anything happens to Hedova.'

'Hedova?'

'That's what we call the girl in the picture. It's short for *Head of a Girl*. Look, here's a photo of my granddaughter. She's called Bindu.' Tia pulls a photo from her wallet and holds it out to Robert.

Still holding the knife in position Robert glances at the girl in the photo. He's sure he's seen her before. She was in the same room as Samuel when he was taking photos. That's it! She looked him straight in the face as if to say, you're not allowed to do that. So she's upset because her favourite picture has disappeared, is she?

Robert can hear his dad's voice. 'Screw the big institutions for as much as you can get but never hurt the little guy.' Or little girl in this case. Robert lets the picture slide to the floor. In the movies Tia would put out her hand at this point and say, give me the knife or gun or whatever the weapon is, and Robert would hand it over and start to cry. But this isn't the movies and Robert still has the knife and there's no sign of tears.

The doorbell rings.

Robert looks at Tia, startled. 'You've called the police!'

Tia shakes her head. 'We haven't told the police anything. It could be someone from the gallery come to check I'm okay. I've been here a long time and they'll be worried.'

Robert peers through the spyhole. 'I know him. He was at the railway station.' He turns to Tia. 'Were you there too?'

She nods.

'And that's Jamie! What's Jamie got to do with this?'

Robert listens intently as Tia gives a brief account of how Jamie's winning tickets led them to Robert's flat. The bell rings again, more urgently than before. Robert lays the knife back on the glass table. He checks his reflection in the mirror then opens the door.

'You'd better come in.'

Douglas pushes past Robert and within seconds is at Tia's side.

'Thank God you're not hurt.'

The intensity of Douglas's relief surprises Tia and yet it stops short of an embrace. At this moment that's what she needs, to be held tight until she stops trembling.

Douglas spots Hedova lying abandoned on the floor. 'Is she...?'

'She's fine. No damage.'

Douglas almost sobs with relief. Tia wonders what he would have done if Robert had actually cut the canvas.

'You can take the frigging picture. I never want to see

it again,' Robert says. He looks at Hedova with loathing. 'She's just a spoilt brat. I can't see why anyone thinks she's beautiful.'

Tia catches Douglas's eye, begging him not to take the bait.

It doesn't take her long to persuade Douglas it's not necessary to call in the police. She points out that Robert doesn't pose a risk to anyone (Tia decides neither the fist in her face nor the blade pressed into the canvas deserves a mention) and Jamie is happy to fall in line. Jamie has developed quite a soft spot for Robert and wouldn't want to see him behind bars.

The difficult bit is trying to convince the director, by phone, that as they have regained possession of the picture without paying a single penny in ransom, it's in nobody's interest to press charges. Robert has learnt his lesson and it's extremely unlikely he'll repeat the offence. Eventually they win him round; it's only a provisional agreement, he warns, until he has time to consult the board of governors. Douglas is pretty sure he can influence the governors to drop any idea of prosecution.

'I have a favour to ask of you,' Robert says. 'Any chance I could have my scarf back? Only it was my dad's.'

Douglas says he'll do his best. They wrap the picture securely and prepare to leave.

Robert says, 'Will you keep in touch? I'd like to hear what Bindu says when she sees the picture hanging where it belongs.' In spite of the fact she tricked him, Robert has taken a shine to Tia. Tia warns Robert this is not a good idea and Douglas backs her up. Robert understands. They don't want a loser like him hanging around.

Jamie volunteers to carry the picture down to Tia's car. Robert stands in the doorway looking utterly forlorn. It occurs to Jamie that Robert would make an ideal subject for his research into the social construction of the criminal mind. Jamie is on course for a first and a series of interviews with Robert would give an edge to his dissertation that might just clinch it.

He calls out, 'I'll be back in a moment, mate. Don't close the door. You look as if you could use some company.'

Robert grins. This is exactly the kind of thing friends say to each other. From now on Jamie qualifies as his friend.

While Tia and Douglas drive back to the gallery, at a more sedate pace than when they came, Tia provides a blow-by-blow account of what happened in Robert's flat. Rehearsing the twists and turns, she realises how brave she was to march in there alone and how clever to squeeze a confession out of him. Douglas listens in silence until Tia runs out of words.

'You missed something out.'

'Pardon?'

'The knife. You didn't mention he had a knife.'

'Okay. He had a Stanley knife but he wasn't planning to use it on me. It was to cut the canvas with.'

'All the same, I shouldn't have let you go in there alone.'

'Let me? You couldn't have stopped me!'

'I should have tried. I'd never forgive myself if anything happened to you.'

She should be annoyed that he feels responsible for her, implying she can't take care of herself, but she isn't; she loves it that he's so concerned.

'Nothing did happen so you can stop worrying.'

'I don't think I can. I always worry about people I like.'

Tia knows she should reciprocate but can't find the words. Instead she rests her hand lightly on his arm.

Douglas lets it stay a few moments then replaces it on the steering wheel, gently so that it doesn't feel like a rebuff.

'How did you pass your driving test?'

They both laugh.

She says, 'Poor Robert. I hope he'll be alright.'

'Why poor Robert? He's very lucky we didn't hand him over to the police.'

'He didn't have much of a childhood. He showed me a photograph. I don't think his parents took much interest in him.'

It occurs to Tia that Subir and Robert are roughly the same age. But that's where the comparison ends. Robert had none of the privileges Subir enjoyed – private school, no shortage of money, educated and supportive parents. Hang on, make that supportive mother; Subir's father wasn't sober long enough to support anyone. And the fraught atmosphere at home must have made it difficult for Subir to concentrate on his studies. So perhaps the comparison is not as straightforward as it appears.

Douglas says, 'I thought you didn't believe in taking circumstances into account.'

'I'm not sure what to think.'

Will –	*Have you heard the latest? They found Hedova! She's on her way home!*
Bess –	*Who found her?*
Will –	*Douglas. With Tia's help no doubt. I always knew he would.*
Bess –	*Siegfried! Did you hear what Will said? Your sweetheart is coming back.*
Amy –	*What's that?*
Bess –	*Hedova is on her way home. Siegfried! Have you nothing to say?*

Siegfried – *She's very young, don't you think? Too young for me. I'll be glad to see her of course and I shall continue to be her friend, but nothing more. My heart is captured by another.*

Amy – *He means me. I'm sure he means me.*

Bess – *Shame on you both! Couldn't you be faithful for just one week? Poor Hedova. She'll be overjoyed to see us again only to discover her beloved has betrayed her.*

Amy – *Overjoyed? I've never seen her look anything but miserable.*

Elizabeth – *Not half as miserable as I do but then I have good cause.*

Will – *No one is allowed to be miserable today.*

Bess – *What happens to Douglas and Tia now, once they have brought Hedova safely home? Will they still see each other?*

Will – *I'm sure they will. And I have a feeling we'll be seeing much less of Douglas from now on.*

CHAPTER NINE

It's just a week since Douglas and Tia began their investigation and what a week it's been! No one believes the cover story anymore but nor do they know the full sequence of events. Setting up the Volunteers' Room as their HQ, sitting through hours of CCTV footage, the bizarre phone calls from Robert, the breakthrough with the purple felt tip and the raffle ticket only to be disappointed, the failed attempt to pay a ransom, Jamie's unexpected visit supplying the vital link, the subsequent race across the city and highly charged encounter with Robert.

Tia suggests they organise a simple ceremony to mark Hedova's return and to say thank you to the people who helped find her. Keep it low-key and hold it first thing, before the gallery gets busy.

'Who shall we invite? The director, his PA, Lucy, Evie, Julie, the caretaker and Jamie. And Bindu of course, even if it means taking her out of school for an hour or two. Have I forgotten anyone?'

To Tia's surprise Douglas doesn't make a joke about inviting Bess and Will.

Julie comes in early to help set things up. It's her day off but she doesn't want to miss the occasion. She brings her daughter Mia with her because Mia's school heating system is on the blink and the staff refuse point blank to teach in freezing classrooms. While Tia and Julie arrange cups and glasses and serviettes, Bindu and Mia size each other up with a view to making friends; neither wants to make the first move in case she's rejected.

Although strictly speaking the event is by invitation only, the word gets round and the Portrait Room is pretty much packed. Tia hands out glasses of fruit juice, Evie follows in her wake with plates of home-made biscuits and cheesy nibbles; tea and coffee are available outside on the balcony.

Tia looks round for Bindu and Mia but can't see them. She calls softly and then more stridently but the girls don't appear. Douglas, who is introducing Jamie to the delights of the Portrait Room, offers to round them up. When five minutes later he still hasn't returned, Tia and Julie go to join the hunt. They pass a group of visitors on their way upstairs and Tia asks if they have seen a couple of seven-year-old girls. They haven't. Tia asks if they've seen a white-haired gentleman looking for a couple of seven-year-old girls. They laugh and say no, they haven't seen him either!

Douglas is in the foyer. 'I don't know where else to look.'

Tia asks if he's tried the toilets.

'Evie has. Both sets.'

'The furniture store on level one? That would be a good place to hide.'

'Nope. Didn't think of it. I'll nip up there now.'

And he's off before anyone can stop him. While he's gone Tia checks the cafe. No luck there either. Douglas returns empty-handed. Tia glances at her watch. The director is due to give his speech in five minutes.

'Hasn't anyone seen them this morning?'

'They were in the shop when I arrived,' Tyrone says, 'but they didn't stay long. I checked.'

Douglas and Tia's eyes meet. The stockroom! Bindu was with them when they went to see the scarf and cap. Douglas takes off in the direction of the staff corridor with Tia and Julie hurrying to catch up. Yes! A strip of light shows under the door which, when Douglas tries to open it, appears to be locked. On the second attempt it swings open and there they are, Bindu and Mia, standing side by side, their cheeks tear-stained and their eyes red with crying.

'What on earth are you doing in here?' Julie exclaims.

'We came to have a look at the badges.'

'We were just looking. We weren't going to steal them.'

'You were too going to steal them!'

'Wasn't!'

'Then the door handle stuck and we couldn't get out.'

'She said we were going to die.'

'Well it's true. We could've!'

'It's okay,' Tia says. 'Everything's okay.' She is surprised to find herself on the verge of tears. 'Sorry. Didn't sleep very well last night.' She wipes her eyes and blows her nose.

'You don't need to apologise.' Douglas gives her a quick hug, not the real thing, just a sample to show what he's capable of.

The director raises his hand and the assembled group falls silent. He thanks each person individually for his or her contribution to the successful restoration of *Head of a Girl* to her home in the Whitler Gallery. He says nothing about the identity of the thief but confesses the journey leading to Hedova's rescue hasn't been easy.

'Douglas and Tia have done a magnificent job as detectives! I'd recommend them to anyone. In fact that's not a bad idea. Why don't the two of you go into partnership and set up your own agency? I'd give you a cracking reference.' The suggestion is greeted with laughter. 'Now let's get on with the main business.'

The senior curator appears with the picture, the director removes the cover with a flourish and the caretaker fastens Hedova to the wall. Loud clapping, Tia's cue to propose a non-alcoholic toast (the director refused to sanction bubbly at this hour of the morning).

'I give you Hedova, a young woman originally from seventeenth-century Europe, and now a much-loved member of our Whitler family. Welcome home! And please could you try to look a little more cheerful?'

Laughter and more applause. They break into small groups now the ceremony is over. Tia looks around for Douglas. He's huddled in a corner with Bindu and Mia. Then suddenly Bindu is walking towards her carrying the most enormous bouquet. For no logical reason Tia is close to tears for the second time that day. She passes the flowers to Evie while she gathers Bindu to her breast and holds her tight.

'I've told Daddy I'm not going to the childminder anymore. I want to spend every holiday with you and Douglas uncle. That's all right isn't it Thakuma?'

The director poses in front of the picture. He needs an illustration to go with the article he's written for the local press describing the gallery's resilience when targeted by the criminal underclass. Tia takes some shots of Bindu having a one-to-one with Hedova and some of Bindu and Mia pulling funny faces.

Will –   *How lovely to see you again, my dear.*
Bess –   *If only she could tell us where she's been.*
Hedova –   *Cemetery*
Will –   *She spoke!*
Bess –   *I didn't hear her.*
Will –   *Try again, Hedova. Tell us where you've been.*
Hedova –   *In a cemetery. I slept in someone's grave. And then I slept under Robert's bed.*
Bess –   *She can speak! Siegfried! Amy! Elizabeth! Hedova can speak!*
Elizabeth – *Did they look after you? Is there any damage?*
Amy –   *Who is Robert and what were you doing in his bedroom?*
Bess –   *Tell us what you saw. Tell us what it's like outside.*
Will –   *You must be exhausted.*
Hedova –   *Yes. Very tired.*
Will –   *You should rest.*
Hedova –   *I will do, and then I'll tell you my news. I know who I am! It all came back to me when I was lying in the grave.*
Amy –   *I knew it! You're a princess or maybe an empress disguised as a servant. Am I right?*
Will –   *Can't you see she's exhausted? We've waited fifty years, it won't hurt us to wait a little longer.*

The director excuses himself; he has to finish putting together a funding bid. One by one the others follow his example and drift back to their desks. Tia and Julie clear the debris and stack the borrowed items on the trolley. Douglas gives them a hand then wanders over to inspect Hedova. He occupies his customary seat on the upholstered bench facing Will and Bess. Tia goes over to join him.

'I assume they're pleased to have her back?'

He chuckles. 'I haven't asked but I imagine they would be.'

'So what are you asking them?'

'I'm not asking, I'm telling.'

'Okay so what are you telling them?' She can barely conceal her irritation.

'That I'm grateful for their help. And that I think I can manage without them from now on.' His eyes are surprisingly bright and clear for a man of his age. More green than blue. Tia hasn't noticed before.

'How come? I mean, what changed?'

'I decided I'd rather spend my time with the living than the dead.'

Tia wonders whether Douglas is referring to his dead wife or the dead subjects of the portraits or both. But that's not important, is it? What really matters is who he means by 'the living'.

'You remember when we took Bindu out to the Whinnies, you asked if I had found a new partner after my wife died?'

Tia nods.

'And I said I'd never do that. Well, I might have changed my mind.'

He doesn't look at Tia as he says this, as if he wants to make it clear this is a general statement rather than referring to his relationship with her in particular.

The council house clock strikes half ten. Douglas sighs. 'Is that the time? I should get back to my desk. Start clearing the backlog.'

'And I promised to get Bindu to school as soon as we're done.'

An hour or so later, with Bindu safely back in the classroom, Tia heads for the peace and quiet of her basement office. Visitors often compare being in the archives with being in a submarine or a bank vault or even a mausoleum, but to Tia it's cosy and it's home. Every item in her office is personalised, from the little bamboo stool she sat on as a child and now uses as a footrest, to the wonky mug without a handle she made at pottery evening class.

She logs into her laptop and runs through the emails, deletes as many as possible, responds immediately to the straightforward ones and adds the rest to her to-do list. She manages to keep going for an hour or so before succumbing to temptation. Putting everything to one side, including Subir's anticipated disapproval, she types Private Investigator into the search engine.

The idea that she and Douglas could join forces as private investigators occurred to Tia before the director mentioned it, but she didn't think of it as a serious option. Now she is back at her desk it seems the only way forward if she is to avoid dying of boredom! Having sampled something of life as an investigator she's hungry for more. And if she's honest, she wants more of Douglas too; as a fellow investigator that is, a close colleague. Nothing more. Not yet anyway.

'Douglas? Can you come down to archives when you've got a moment? There's something I'd like to discuss.'

'I am intrigued! Be with you as soon as I can.'

While Tia is making coffee, Douglas trawls through the publications on her shelves. He shivers and rubs his palms together to generate some heat.

'It's freezing! How do you manage to get any work done at this temperature?'

Tia passes him a shawl. 'Here, put this round your shoulders and you'll soon warm up.'

He can't work out what to do with the folds of cloth so she wraps him up like a parcel and steers him towards a chair. Douglas cradles his mug of coffee, warming his frozen fingers while he waits for her to begin.

'I've been thinking about what the director said. You know, you and me setting up as private investigators.' Her left foot is jiggling furiously.

'I rather think he was joking!'

'Maybe, but I'm not.'

Douglas pulls the shawl closer so it bunches up round his neck. 'I agree, finding Hedova was fun. But I don't want to spend my time spying on divorcing couples and benefit cheats and false insurance claimants. That's what most private investigators do, isn't it?'

'Most of them, yes. But we can choose to specialise. We can stick to retrieving stolen property, for example. We've proved we're good at that.' Tia can tell from Douglas's expression that he's tempted. 'We'll call ourselves Bindu Detective Bureau. Shortened to BDB for the logo.'

'Has a good ring to it.' Douglas picks up a pen and writes the name across a sheet of A4. 'We need a strapline. Alliteration always works well. How about "Dependable and Discreet"?' He experiments with different designs.

Tia says, 'We can work from home to begin with.'

'Then when business picks up and our client base expands we can rent office space and appoint a receptionist.' Douglas draws a figure with earphones sitting behind a desk while a queue of matchstick customers wait their turn.

'Tia laughs. '*Gachche kantal ghonphe tel!*'

'I beg your pardon?'

'A proverb. Literally, the jackfruit is still in the tree but the owner is already rubbing oil into his moustache.'

Douglas looks bewildered. He can't see the connection between a jackfruit and a moustache. Tia explains that jackfruit are very sticky and can only be washed out of a moustache if it has been oiled in advance.

'Ah! In other words, "don't count your chickens before they hatch". You're quite right. We're getting ahead of ourselves. Let's sleep on it and talk again tomorrow.'

Tia helps Douglas extricate himself from the shawl.

'One more thing before you go.' Tia isn't sure how Douglas will take this but she's determined to try. 'We'll be the brains of the outfit, you and me, but we could do with a younger pair of eyes and legs to do the groundwork. I thought about asking Robert...'

'You do surprise me. Dependable and discreet are not the first words that come to mind when describing Robert!'

'We can send him for training. They do all sorts of courses. I've had a look.'

Douglas suggests they put Robert as an agenda item for their first meeting.

Tia folds the shawl and hangs it over the back of her chair. 'What happened to sleeping on it?'

'There's no point. I can see how determined you are. And to be honest the idea has been growing on me for a while. I would have suggested it myself, only you got there first.'

'We need some ground rules. Equal partners. All decisions taken jointly. I'll throw a few ideas together.'

Douglas rests his hands on Tia's shoulders and looks into her eyes. He pulls her towards him and kisses her lightly on the cheek.

'Shall we discuss it over dinner?'

* * *

Hedova – *My real name is Angelica. I was born in Florence where my father Filippo Furini, was a portrait painter. My brother Francesco and sister Alessandra sat at his feet while he taught* disegno *and* colorito. *They were always on the lookout for new subjects to paint. On one occasion when my mother was not at home they stripped me of my fine gown and ornaments and dressed me as a pauper. As if he wished to humiliate me further, my brother invited the other apprentices to join them. Wearing only a cotton shift which barely concealed my limbs, I found myself the unwilling object of close scrutiny by many pairs of eyes.*

Bess – *You poor dear.*

Hedova – *When she discovered what they had done my mother showed the canvases to my father who ordered them to be cleaned for reuse, except one which he judged to possess a peculiar beauty and* therefore worthy of preservation. That painting is what you see before you now.

Will –   Were they punished for what they'd done?

Hedova –   In a manner of speaking. After the incident my brother was dispatched to the studio of Matte Roselli, and Alessandra studied under a private tutor who came to the house.

Amy –   And what became of Angelica?

Hedova –   I showed no aptitude for painting but I loved music and had a sweet voice. I had the good fortune to become a singer in the court of Cosimo II de Medici, Grand Duke of Tuscany.

Will –   And now you have your voice back, we look forward to hearing you sing!